# Realms of the Dragons

Maiden to the Dragon, Book 2

Mac Flynn

All names, places, and events depicted in this book are fictional and products of the author's imagination.

No part of this publication may be reproduced, stored in a retrieval system, converted to another format, or transmitted in any form without explicit, written permission from the publisher of this work. For information regarding redistribution or to contact the author, write to the publisher at the following address.

Crescent Moon Studios, Inc.
P.O. Box 117
Riverside, WA 98849

Website: www.macflynn.com
Email: mac@macflynn.com

ISBN / EAN-13: 9781791934491

Copyright © 2018 by Mac Flynn

Second Edition

## CONTENTS

Chapter 1..................................................1
Chapter 2................................................10
Chapter 3................................................16
Chapter 4................................................22
Chapter 5................................................30
Chapter 6................................................38
Chapter 7................................................46
Chapter 8................................................53
Chapter 9................................................59
Chapter 10..............................................66
Chapter 11..............................................73
Chapter 12..............................................79
Chapter 13..............................................88
Chapter 14..............................................94
Chapter 15..............................................99
Chapter 16............................................106
Chapter 17............................................112

Continue the adventure...................................117
Other series by Mac Flynn............................125

# CHAPTER 1

The life of a Maiden to a dragon didn't seem so glamorous. Actually, at that moment it was downright miserable.

"A warm fire. An electric blanket. A roof over my head."

That was my dream mantra as our group of two dozen riders rode through a torrential rain. All around us was a world of mud and thick forest. We were three days out from the High Castle, and ahead of us was another four days of outdoor fun. The dirt road we traveled on was now a mud pit fit for any hog. My cloak was soaked through and there were two puddles always with me, one in each of my riding boots.

I could barely see ten feet in front of my horse's nose, and what I saw I didn't like. More rain. "A warm fire. An electric-"

"Do you know how to create electricity?" Xander, my personal dragon lord, asked me. He rode close beside me, and in front of us were half our guards. Behind us were the other half along with a few servants and our two friends, Stephanie and Cayden.

I raised my hooded head and arched an eyebrow at my dragon lord. "Do you even know what electricity is?"

He smiled and gave a nod. "Yes. Darda spoke often of your world when she first came into my mother's service. Her tales of electricity, power without physical force, have stayed with me."

"She's from my world?" I asked him.

He nodded. "Yes. The Portal is always open, and because of that people have been known to fall through. The rules demanded she not return to warn others, and so she was pressed into the service of the priests of the Portal until she was given to my mother."

I glanced over my shoulder at the short woman who followed behind us. Her stooped servile posture and primitive attire didn't bespeak of a person from my world. Still, that did explain her talk to we girls in the stable and about what we were leaving behind.

"So how long ago did she stumble into this place?" I asked him.

"Nearly sixty years ago."

I winced. That was a long time without electricity.

Xander stared ahead and pursed his lips. "I have long wished to see this magic of your world, and that is why I asked if you have knowledge enough to create this electricity."

I shook my head. "Nope, not a thing. I doubt I could create an electric shock by dragging my feet, much less enough that could power a light bulb or something simple like that."

Xander looked ahead of us and a small smile played across his lips. "Then I still must continue my dream."

I felt a little guilty at having dashed his hopes. "Maybe you can go there some day," I suggested.

He shook his head. "That is not possible. You yourself witnessed what would happen were I to even touch the Portal's surface."

"But I got through," I reminded him.

Xander returned his gaze to me and studied me. "Yes, but you are the first. I should not consider myself an exception to a rule that has stood a thousand years."

I wrinkled my nose. "So how come I'm an exception?"

He shook his head. "That is a mystery the priests could not solve and our books could not answer for us. However-" A teasing smile played across his lips, "-I would not have you make the attempt again."

I raised my head and saluted him. The raindrops nearly drowned me. "I promise I'll be a good little Maiden."

He chuckled. "I expect you to be something other than that, but I would ask nothing else of you."

I smiled, but the smile soon faded. Thinking about what I left behind reminded me of the rain. I huddled inside my wet cloak and shivered as the damp sank into my bones. The forest around us seemed so vast, and I felt like just a tiny, wet little speck in it.

Xander pulled his horse closer to mine and reached behind himself for his travel blanket. He let go of his reigns to drape the blanket across my shivering shoulders. The weight of the thick woolen blanket was preceded by the heat it trapped inside me.

I grabbed the front-top edges to keep the blanket on my slick shoulders and smiled at him. "Thanks." I glanced around us at the tall forest with its thick-trunked trees and undergrowth. "It feels like we've been in this place forever. How much farther do we have to go before we get out of this place?"

"The Viridi Silva is one of the largest forests in our world. We won't reach its southern boundary for another two days," he told me.

Xander looked at the guards ahead of us. Their heads were topped with rounded metal helmets and their hands were hidden by thick leather gloves with holes at the ends. They wore silver armor covered in cloaks, but I could see the armor had slits in the back near their shoulder blades. The look was similar to what the priest of the Portal had, and I knew what that meant.

"Are there any humans in this world besides the ones from mine?" I asked him.

Xander nodded. "Yes, but their settlements are few and far between. Many mated with dragons long ago and the dragon blood overrode their human line. Others have simply faded into history."

I glanced over my shoulder at Darda and Stephanie. "So we're kind of an endangered species here."

"I am afraid that is very close to the truth," he agreed. He straightened in his saddle and cleared his throat. "Spiros!"

The helmet of one of the guards was more elaborate than the others. Rather than a smooth top, his had a crest like the spine on a dragon's tail. He pulled his reigns back and turned toward us. The man was about thirty with a scar across his left cheek. His face was marred with care, but the corners of his lips had a hint of a smile. There was also a twinkle in his eyes that reminded me of Xander.

"You called, My Lord?" he shouted back.

Xander nodded. "Yes. I wish for your presence at my side for a moment." Spiros gave a few brief instructions to a young man of twenty who traveled at his side before he galloped over and joined us. Xander gestured to me. "I haven't properly introduced you to my Maiden. Miriam, this is my captain, Spiros."

His barely-concealed smile appeared as he bowed his head to me. "It is an honor to meet you, My Lady."

I nodded. "Ditto."

"Spiros and I grew up together, so do not be alarmed if he appears too impertinent," Xander warned me.

"If I am impertinent it is because I feel my advice will do you some good, My Lord," Spiros countered.

Xander chuckled. "Do me good? As when you coaxed me into riding my father's finest bull to see if its name of 'Devil' befitted it?"

"You rode him very well, My Lord, and no one doubted your bravery afterward," his captain argued.

"But some doubted very much I would survive my injuries," Xander pointed out.

I raised an eyebrow, all my discomfort forgotten. "Did the bull gore you?"

Spiro leaned forward so I could see him as he shook his head. "No, My Lady. The old king, My Lord's father, beat him quite profusely."

Xander winced at the memory and rubbed his arm. "I am ashamed to say I deserved as much. In riding the bull I had broken his strict order to stay away from the beast."

"So you see, My Lady, My Lord is in great need of my counsel to save him from his rash decisions," Spiros commented.

I snorted. "With friends like you who needs enemies?"

Spiros chuckled. "A very interesting saying, My Lady. I shall have to remember it."

"And wear it as a badge of honor, no doubt," Xander teased him. He leaned toward his friend and studied him with a sharp eye. "Though on the subject of good advice, I do recall your attempt to fly over the Grand Canal before your wings were softened."

"Softened?" I asked him.

"The wings of a dragon child are at first very hard and brittle," he explained to me. "The exposure of the wings to air and exercise softens the muscles and allows them to spread to their full length."

"If you will recall, My Lord, my father would not allow me to enter knight training until my wings were softened," Spiros spoke up. "I sought to show him that they had softened, at least far enough to support me."

Xander chuckled. "They had softened enough for you to fall into the Canal and nearly drowned yourself. If my guard escort had not found to where we had eluded them we would not be having this discussion."

I looked from Xander to Spiros. "You guys got away from the guards?"

Spiros's mischievous eyes flickered to his lord. "My Lord was very adept at eluding his keepers."

Any more conversation was cut off by a sudden worsening of the already-worse weather. The torrential rains fell faster and drowned out more than just the primitive road. I could barely hear myself think much less overhear the conversation between the two old friends. What I did catch, however, was a change in their expressions. They gazed out on the rains with pursed lips and furrowed brows before they glanced at each other with knowing looks. Spiros bowed his head and trotted off to retake his position at the head of the guards.

Cayden filled the empty spot vacated by Spiros, and Stephanie came up on his left side. "What do you make of this weather?" he shouted above the pounding rains.

Xander shook his head. "We cannot journey much farther than the bridge."

"If the bridge is to be had," Cayden pointed out.

There was no use talking at the top of our lungs, so the next couple of minutes was devoid of all but the thunderous rains that fell around us. The muddy road opened up ahead of us and revealed a small river. At least, small when there wasn't a flood warning. As we approached the waters I could hear the roar of the stream as it turned over the rocks in its bed and swept away the trees that lined its banks.

The bridge was a wooden makeup of logs strapped together with heavy rope and sealed with a tar-looking substance. Thick trees as wide as I was tall were the support beams that forced the bridge to curve over the water in a gentle arch. Below the arch were the fast waters of the wild river. I winced every time I heard a tree or rock slam into one of those pillars.

Spiros stopped his guards at the edge of the bridge. Xander trotted forward to stand beside his old friend and I cautiously followed. "I do not like this, My Lord," the captain shouted above the pounding rain.

Xander pursed his lips as he studied the bridge. The thick logs swayed side to side at each knock of their pillars. "We have little choice. There is no other bridge."

"Then allow my men and I to cross and test the logs, My Lord," Spiros pleaded.

Xander shook his head. "There is no time. The bridge may collapse at any moment. We cross now." He turned his horse so he rode perpendicular to the line and stood on his stirrups so all could see him. "We cross at once! Make two lines at two abreast and follow the rider in front of you!"

The riders grouped themselves into the long lines. I clutched my reigns and tensed my legs against the body of the horse. My steed threw its head back and whinnied.

Xander sidled up to my horse and leaned close to me. "Would you rather ride with me?"

I managed a shaky smile. "And miss all this fun? Not on your life."

He glanced past me at the roaring water beneath the bridge and frowned. I hardly heard his murmured words. "I pray not."

That's when an ear-splitting roar bashed my ears. I whipped my head to the left and upstream of the bridge. A huge tree with a six-foot trunk floated on the currents of the white-water waves.

"Across!" Xander yelled.

Too late. The tree bore down on the bridge, and us. It slammed into the left side and sank deep into the thick timbers. Many of the horses whinnied and reared up. My horse wasn't an exception. It reared up on both its back legs. One of the two remaining hooves slipped on the thick logs. The horse staggered backward and into the downstream wall. We hit it hard. I couldn't keep my position on the slick saddle and fell into the roaring abyss of the wild river.

# CHAPTER 2

The cold water enveloped me in its harsh embrace. I was taken by the current and swept downstream away from the bridge. The water tumbled me head-over-heels until I didn't know up from down. My shoulder slammed into a large boulder. The force made me yell. My air bubbles floated from my mouth and into the dark abyss. Water flooded my lungs. I kicked and paddled, but without knowing which way to go I fell deeper into the watery depths.

I was on the verge of losing consciousness when I saw a far-off blue light. The light was a thin strip that swam through the water like an eel. It flitted around me like a playful dolphin and stopped in front of me. Its warm glow spread beyond its body and enveloped me. I felt like a soft blanket had fallen on me.

There was also the air. I took a deep breath and breathed in a big gulp of the precious oxygen. The glow also protected me from the current. I remained floating while the water streamed past me.

The body of the light flitted back and stopped in front of me. It formed itself into the shape of a man of forty with a beard of and dark blue eyes like the darkness around me. He had blue skin and wore a toga down to his waist. Beyond his waist was a tail like that of the legendary mermaid, or in his case a merman.

He smiled at me, and the soft warmth around me greater heavier. "Good evening, Young Niece. What has brought you to my waters?"

I swallowed the lump in my throat. "I-I kind of fell in."

He chuckled. The blue glow pulsed in and out with his mirth. "A very truthful answer, Niece." He tilted his head back and looked up. "Your companions are searching for you. One young man seems especially distraught at your disappearance."

I whipped my head back and swept my eyes over the darkness above me. There was no sign of the surface, much less the people he mentioned. I turned back to the strange man and started back.

The merman swam closer to me so our faces were only a few inches apart. His blue eyes reminded me of those that belonged to the Lady of the Water. They caught me in their soft, caring depths as he brushed his palm against my cheek. It was like being touched by the strong current. "Take care, Niece. The forest is not what it once was. Even the skies are not safe."

The light around me pulled me away from the strange creature and upward. The merman cupped his hands over his mouth and leaned toward me. "And improve your swimming!" He waved to me before he turned back into his eel form and swam away.

The light carried me up to the bank and within two feet of the surface before it faded. The swift, unforgiving current of the river pushed against me. I paddled and kicked with all my might, and in a few seconds I broke through to the stormy night air. A hand snatched one of my wrists and pulled me onto the bank.

I was spread out on the ground and onto my back. Xander's ashen face hovered over mine. Behind him stood Stephanie and Cayden. Stephanie's wet cheeks were streaked with salt water.

I managed a small smile at my dragon lord. "Next time I'll ride with you."

Xander's expression softened and I even saw a ghost of a smile as he lifted me into his arms. He stood and turned away from the river bank to where the others stood beneath the canopy of trees. We were about ten yards down from the half-broken bridge. Everyone else had made it safely across, and Spiros held the reigns of my treacherous horse.

Xander carried me up the short, gentle slope to the safety of the trees. The rain was not so heavy now, but that didn't help to dry out our wet group.

"Let us make camp," Xander ordered his captain.

Spiros bowed his head and half-turned to the troops and servants. "Break for camp!"

Galen, Xander's personal physician, came up to us and bowed his head. "Would you like me to treat My Lady?"

Xander shook his head. "No, I do not believe there is anything serious enough to warrant your skills, Galen. I will see to what bruises she has."

Xander carried me over to a fallen log and set me down, and our two friends followed us. The guards staked out a leather canopy over our heads and he knelt in front of me. His eyes and hands searched me. His eyes flickered up to me. "How did you come to the surface?"

I winced when he touched my bruised shoulder. "I wish I knew. I fell in the water and this glowing guy came out of nowhere. He told me I needed to practice my swimming and sent me back up."

Xander paused and tilted his head back to look at me. "A glowing man?"

I nodded. "Yeah. He kind of reminded me of the lady around the High Castle except he had a fish tail."

"It sounds like you met the spirit of the river," Cayden spoke up.

Xander looked up at his young friend and a small, mischievous smile danced across his lips. "Surely your extensive book-learning has taught you the name of the spirit."

Cayden furrowed his brow. "I believe it was the same name as the river, Potami. He was rumored to be a half fish-half man of minor god of the waters in this area, but the tales of him are quite old. Some have even doubted he exists."

"His tail looked pretty real to me," I quipped.

"What do the tales say of him?" Stephanie spoke up.

Cayden stood a little taller at his lady's inquiry and smiled. "Many of the tales center around his mischievous nature. He was known to drag maidens to the deepest waters of the river, to parts protected by his magic and currents. There he would woo them and, well-" he paused and a blush slipped onto his cheeks. Stephanie eagerly awaited more of his story, so he straightened and coughed into his hand. "He would woo and wed them in a-um, in a cursory fashion, and once finished he would return them to the surface. It is said he charmed dragon, man and elf into his waters."

Stephanie's face lit up with curiosity. "Elf?"

He nodded. "Yes. The elves inhabit the larger forests of our world."

Stephanie swept her eyes over the trees around us. "Even here?"

"Especially here, though even an elf wouldn't be caught in such a storm as this," Cayden told her.

Xander returned his attention to me and studied me with his bright green eyes. "And yet you returned to me unscathed by his amorous history."

I wrinkled my nose. "Water guys really aren't my thing. Besides, he kept calling me 'niece,' so anything beyond a peck on the cheek was going to be really weird."

My dragon lord raised an eyebrow. "'Niece?'"

I shrugged. "Beats me. Maybe it was his way of telling me I wasn't his type."

Xander smiled. "You are better suited to the skies than to the rivers."

I looked up and winced as a few stray drops from my hear bounced off my nose. "Maybe I'll just keep my feet on the dry ground for a while." I glanced around at all the puddles that littered the forest floor. "Speaking of ground, do I have to watch where I step around here, or do these water gods stick to bigger puddles of water?"

"They only inhabit permanent waters," Cayden assured me.

Xander stood and looked over the campsite that the guards slowly erected. A half dozen large leather canvases were tied to the trunks and stretched between the trees. Darda and a few other servants gathered what dry leaves and needles they could and spread them on the ground. Some of the men fetched firewood while others gathered stones and placed them in a circle.

I stood and looked to Stephanie before I jerked my head toward the leaf gathering. "How about you and I give them a hand?"

Xander set his hand on my shoulder and shook his head. "They would not wish for your assistance."

I glared up at him. "I'm not that bad at picking stuff off the-"

"I do not doubt your gathering skills, but a woman in your position assisting them would make them ashamed of themselves," he told me.

I arched an eyebrow. "Come again?"

He nodded at the women as they diligently worked. "If you assisted them then they would see themselves as having failed to provide for your needs, and for a servant to a dragon lord there is no greater dishonor."

My shoulders slumped and I pursed my lips. "You guys have a lot of weird ideas around here."

He smiled. "You will grow accustomed to them."

## CHAPTER 3

Even without my epic scavenging abilities, in a few minutes we had a fine camp area and a roaring fire blazed far beneath one of the leather canvases. There were even a few walls put up for some privacy where I changed into drier clothes. Dinner was cooked, and afterward Xander and I retired to our little hovel away from home.

The change in clothes made me drier, but it didn't stop the chill that had invaded my body. I shivered atop our bed of leaves and furs. The layer of furs over me didn't do anything to alleviate the damp that clung to my bones.

I glanced over my shoulder at him and lowered my voice to a whisper. "You don't happen to have an on-switch for your fire-breathing, do you?"

I jumped when Xander wrapped his arms around me and pulled me against his chest. His body heat transferred into me and stopped my shivering.

"Will that suffice?" he teased.

I snuggled closer to him. "I suppose." His arms around me stiffened. I looked at him again. His eyes were closed and his breathing was quick and shallow. My eyebrows crashed down. "Is something wrong?"

He spoke through clenched teeth. "Your-movements are very suggestive."

That's when I felt the hard bulge against my rear. A blush heated my cheeks and I turned away from him to compose myself. "You guys really want kids, don't you?"

"That is the purpose for choosing a Maiden."

I furrowed my brow as a thought came to mind. "Speaking of that, how come some of the lords were kind of old. Shouldn't you guys be the same age when you're looking for a Maiden?"

"The Choosing is not performed until all the lords of the previous generation have died," he explained.

I arched an eyebrow. "But don't you guys live a really long time? You told me you were two hundred years old."

A smile curled onto his lips. "You flatter me, but I am over three hundred years old."

"So why did you and all the other old guys wait that long to get a girl?" I persisted.

"The Choosing for all the lords is performed at the same time to decrease the chance anyone from your world may discover our existence, and so that no lord will become greater than any other lord," he told me.

My neck started to ache, so I twisted around so we faced each other. "How would the lord be greater than the other ones with a human?"

His eyes swept up my body and his smile widened. "A Maiden is no mere human to we dragon lords. She means the future of our lineage, and the mother of our children."

I couldn't stop the blush that heated my cheeks. It was another bit of relief to my chilled body. I stared at my covered legs and burrowed myself deeper into the warm furs. "That still doesn't answer my question."

He wrapped his arms around me so I was pressed gently against his chest. "An heir to any realm of the dragons is a treasure to its people, but a possible threat to the other lords. If Maidens were to be chosen at any time the Choosing would tip the balance of power in favor of the fresh bloodline."

I furrowed my brow. "So each heir is more powerful than the previous one?"

He nodded. "Yes. The dragon lords of the past sacrificed their power to create the Portal. Each successive generation replenishes that power."

I leaned my head back and looked into his face. "So when is it scheduled to pass that old dragons?"

He tilted his head to one side and chuckled. "The next generation will achieve what my ancestors sought for so long. Strength without the fear that it shall wane."

I cringed. "That sounds kind of bad."

He arched an eyebrow. "How so?"

I furrowed my brow and looked down at his bare chest. The view was great, but my thoughts weren't. "Well, what's the point of having all that power? What does it give you?"

Xander studied me for a moment before a crooked smile slipped onto his lips. "An excellent answer, and one I wouldn't expect of anyone but my Maiden."

I blinked at him. "Come again?"

He bent down and nuzzled my neck. The sensation wasn't unpleasant. Heck, who am I kidding? I loved it. His soft nose against my neck. The feel of his lips brushing against my flesh. It stimulated some warm urges in me.

"It was a test, my Maiden," he whispered. He paused and pulled away from me to catch my eyes. "No, you are Miriam to me. A woman of spirit, but not greed."

I frowned, and not just because his warm body was farther than mine again. "A test? Why the hell were you testing me?"

He raised a hand and cupped my cheek in his palm. "I must know my mate, and believe that we are of the same mind and spirit. Without that knowledge and trust the union would fail."

My eyebrows crashed down. "And how long is this exam going to take?"

Xander leaned down and captured my lips in a brief, but lust-stirring, kiss. He pulled away and smiled at me. "There is no cause for alarm. The test is over, and you have passed with flying colors."

I leaned away from him and pursed my lips. "Well, maybe I'm not done with my testing of you."

He bowed his head. "What would you have me do, Miriam?"

I looked him up and down. There wasn't that much to complain about. "Your-uh-your nose is just a little crooked. And your posture when you sit down is terrible. And you snore."

He chuckled. "I will have to improve myself, but I feel grateful your list is so short. There have been instances where the Maidens were not pleased with their situation for more than the reasons given to you."

"Like them being old?" I guessed. He nodded. "And when the dragons weren't pleased with their Maiden? Like if I hadn't passed the test?"

"Then they are granted the favor of working in the house of that lord, and another woman is fetched from your former world," he told me.

I raised an eyebrow. "So when does it stop? At the hundredth try?"

He smiled and shook his head. "There is no need for that. The Sus have honed their skills over a millennium and are now very adept at finding women who hold the special scent needed to be a Maiden."

I wrinkled my nose. "'Sus?' 'Scent?' So we smell funny?"

"The Sus are the pig-men who gathered you, and no, your scent is not funny. It is only different from most human women," he corrected me.

"So what does this 'scent' smell like to them?"

"Like my world."

"And that is what exactly?"

He nodded at the surrounding woods. "The world of untouched beauty, of ancient, virgin soil and clear blues skies."

"That sounds like more than one scent," I pointed out.

He chuckled. "Those are the scents of magic. A deep, timeless fragrance from when our worlds were young and innocent, and the gods granted us life."

I looked up at the canvas overhead and listened to the soft pattering of the raindrops. "And where it takes forever to get from Point A to Point B."

"The roads around the High Castle are notoriously unkempt, but those in my kingdom are kinder to the traveler," he assured me.

"So which Dragon Lord do I complain to about the roads here?" I wondered.

A dark cloud crossed his face and his smile slipped off his lips. "That is a story for another, longer night. For now we should get some rest."

My curiosity was piqued, but my aching body told me he was right. I hated that.

Well, until he wrapped his arms around me again and pressed me close to his warm body. His soft voice was the last thing I heard before I slipped into sleep.

"May the gods give you good dreams, Miriam."

# CHAPTER 4

They gave me a pretty damn good sleep until the middle of the night. An annoying tap-tap of rainwater tapped against the top of our canvas roof. I scrunched my eyes shut and shifted, but my aching body joined my aching ears. There was a stiffness in my joints and a heat in my head I didn't like.

I creaked open my eyes and sniffled. My nose dripped like the incessant noise above me. I burrowed myself deeper beneath the furs and glared at Xander's cute chest. "Why didn't I pack some NyQuil?" I muttered to myself.

Xander's bright green eyes stared at me through the darkness. "You have a touch of fever."

My body shook with a slight chill. "You don't happen to have a remedy for stuff like that in this world, do you?

Maybe some of your scales are a quick-cure or maybe you're carrying around a medicine cabinet in one of your bags?"

He shook his head. "No. Unfortunately, dragons do not often catch colds, so a cure is not readily at hand."

I sniffled. "Suddenly this whole coming back thing doesn't seem like such a good idea."

"Do you regret returning to me?" he wondered.

I sighed and shook my head. "No, but I could really go for the four-star treatment right now."

Xander wrapped his arms around me and pressed me close to his chest. "I am unsure what the 'four-star' treatment is, but this may improve your health."

His warm body soothed my chills. I leaned my cheek against his chest and closed my eyes as a small smile played across my lips. "This isn't bad."

A high-pitched whistle sounded from outside. Xander sat up and took me and the furs with him. His body tensed as he whipped his head to the canvas doorway.

"Remain here," he ordered me as he stood.

"What is it? What's wrong?" I asked him. Feet pounded by our bedroom and I heard hushed voices not too far off.

He shook his head while he dressed himself. I noticed he didn't neglect a bit of breastplate armor. "The whistle is the call of the watchman. I must go see what is the matter."

Xander rushed out. My aching body complained as I climbed to my feet. I wrapped the furs tightly around myself and shuffled to the front flap. The foot-pounding stopped as I pulled aside the canvas and looked out.

Three-quarters of our guards were amassed at the far end of the small camp with their swords and lances drawn. The remaining soldiers were placed as a second guard in the camp. Xander and Cayden were at the head of the lead guards with Spiros at their side. The dragon lords didn't hold any weapons, but their hands were all they needed. Their fingers with partially transformed into thick, stubby claws that ended in nails that were several inches long. They all held a defensive position with their backs to the camp. The group of dragon-men held very still and stared into the darkness of the surrounding forest.

I leaned forward and squinted. A few dancing yellow lights in the distance caught my attention. The lights were in pairs set close together, and they leapt from side to side through the dark forest. The sound of soft, padded feet came to my ears.

That's when I saw to what the lights and sounds belonged to. The lights were actually yellow eyes, and they were positioned squarely in the long faces of dozens of wolf creatures. The gray, short-haired beasts were the size of a large man. They raced through the trees on all four legs in great leaps and bounds like giant rabbits. Their faces were stretched into snouts and their claws buried themselves deep into the trees to give them more liftoff for the next leap.

"They are werewolves."

I turned to my left and saw Darda approach me. She was wrapped tight in a shawl and heavy cloak.

I stared at her with an arched brow. "*Real* werewolves?"

She stopped beside me and nodded. "Yes. The beasts are common in the darker places of this world, but I have never seen-"

"Prepare yourselves!" Spiros shouted.

The werewolves barreled down on our small unit of guards. The dragons thrust lance and sword at the beasts and were met by the slashing of claws. Metal clanked against hard nail as the werewolves dove into the line. Half of the beasts went around the line and stampeded into the camp. A small pack of three raced toward us.

"My Lady!" Darda yelled as she pushed me down to the squishy ground.

The earth trembled beneath us as the werewolves trampled the camp grounds. They crashed into the canvas and tore apart the makeshift walls and bedrooms. A young guard with Cayden's colors swept Stephanie from her room a moment before a werewolf slipped on the mud and crashed into the leather wall. It caught in the canvas and thrashed around, tearing the sheet to shreds.

The young guard grabbed his long spear and thrust it mightily into the beast. The werewolf let loose a long, low howl before it fell limp to the ground. I watched in horror as the furry body shrank and revealed a naked man. The clang of metal and sword lessened as the werewolves were either beaten off or killed, leaving a mess of naked bodies behind. The survivors rerouted their stampede and sprinted around the camp.

That's when the sound of a trumpet rang through the forest. The few werewolves remaining broke from battle and, with their tales tucked between their legs, fled into the darkness. Our guards were not unscathed, but they were all still alive. Some of them tensed as another trumpet sounded.

Xander raised one bloodied, clawed hand above him. "Fear not, men! That is the sound of friends!"

Darda climbed off me and wrapped her arms around one of mine. "Forgive me, My Lady. I meant only to save you," she apologized as she helped me up.

I glanced over my shoulder at the ruins of my bedroom and shook my head. "I'm glad you did. I'd rather be muddy than shredded."

Far-off lights in the forest caught my attention. They weren't the paired yellow orbs of the werewolf eyes, but the steady travel of swinging lamps. The tall, elegant shapes of men appeared through the mist. The newcomers walked in four columns of twenty men each. The head of each column held a lamp, and the lamplight glistened off armor.

"Fear not, My Lady," Darda whispered to me as I stiffened. "These are but the Arbor Fae. Elves of the forest."

I snorted and shook my head. "First a river god, then werewolves, now elves? What *isn't* in this world?"

The corner's of Darda's lips curled up. "The fantasies of our old world are the realities of theirs, My Lady."

The march of elvish men reached the edge of our camp and stopped. The elves were attired in gray cloaks that hid most of their thin chest plates. The metal was tinged with green that reflected the forest around us. They covered their feet in thick boots of hide and loose-fitting pants hid their legs. Some had quivers of arrows on their backs, and others held large staffs with spiked tops.

One of them, a man of thirty with pointed ears and shimmering black hair, stepped forward. He was as tall as Xander, but slim and with paler skin. His eyes were the greenish color of fresh moss on a tree trunk and his black hair fell down to his rear. His look was the same as the others but for a single strand of his hair that was braided with green vines and fell across his chest. He was also the only one to carry a sword.

He smiled and bowed his head to Xander and Cayden. "Dragon Lords, I welcome you to the Virea Metsa, and-" he lifted his head and looked past the soldiers at the camp, "-I apologize for your rude reception."

Xander smiled and bowed his head in return. "There is nothing to apologize for, Prince Durion. If anyone has transgressed in this forest, it would be us."

The prince shook his head. "On the contrary, I fear we are very much at fault. You see, we were driving the werewolves away and were not aware you lay in the same direction."

Xander arched an eyebrow. "Driving them away? From the city?"

The humor in the prince's face fled as he gave a nod. "Yes. They sought to attack the city, but we repulsed them and meant to drive them over the bridge."

"You will have a hard time with that. The bridge is nearly ruined," Xander warned him.

The prince looked past him at our little straggling group of travelers. "I fear I am not playing the proper host, and I would rather not dally here too long. Your company is wet and your camp in tatters. Will you not come with us to Keskella and warm yourselves by our hearths?"

Xander bowed his head. "We would like nothing better. Let us gather what we can and we will follow if you will lead."

"My men will help with the gathering," the prince offered as he looked over his shoulder. Without a word from their commander, the men nodded and trudged past their leader and into the camp.

Servants and soldiers alike gathered up the remains of the canvases and the trampled bags. I started when Darda set hr hands on my shoulders and studied my face. "You are deathly pale, My Lady. Will you not take my cloak?"

I smiled and shook my head. That wasn't all that was shaking. My whole body quivered like a leaf. "I-I'm fine. Really."

She pursed her lips and shook her head. "You are not well, My Lady. We must tell My Lord, at least."

Her wish was granted when the dragon lords led the prince over to us. Cayden broke off from them to join Stephanie and her young savior near their destroyed lodgings.

Xander stepped between the prince and me, and gestured to me. "Prince Durion, may I introduce you to my Maiden, Miriam Cait."

The prince smiled and bowed at the waist to me. "It is a pleasure to finally meet the Maiden destined for such a great dragon lord."

"Um, thank-" My reply was interrupted by a violent sneeze.

He raised his head and the humor fled. His eyebrows crashed down as he studied me. "But I fear this exertion has tried your health. You are very unwell."

I rubbed my finger across the opening of my nostrils and shook my head. My voice sounded like a bear that just swallowed a string of hot peppers. "It's just a stupid cold. I'll get over it."

The prince's eyes flickered to Xander. "It would be best if you flew her to Keskella. Your physician is knowledgeable, but in such conditions a warm bed and rest is the best remedy."

"We can't."

Everyone was surprised by the hoarse voice that spoke up. I was the most surprised because it was my voice. I shrank beneath the attention.

"Why can we not?" Xander asked me.

I shrugged. "It's just something that merman told me."

Durion arched an eyebrow. "'Merman?'"

"Miriam met the river god," Cayden spoke up as he joined us with Stephanie at his side.

Xander caught my eyes. "What did he tell you?"

"He told me to be careful in the forest, and that even the skies were dangerous," I revealed.

My dragon lord glanced at Durion. "Is there a threat in the forest?"

The prince pursed his lips, but gave a curt nod. "It is, but the troubles are too long to list here. We should get to Keskella, and once there I will tell you everything."

Xander bowed. "Then we will follow, but on our horses."

# CHAPTER 5

The bodies of the werewolves were buried and the camp, or what remained of it, was duly gathered up. Everything, including us, was packed on the horses.

Xander helped me onto my steed and I winced when my sore rear complained. "Do these things come with an additional padding option?"

He smiled, but I noticed the corners of his mouth showed strain. "I will see what can be done once we reach my kingdom. The saddlers in Alexandria are some of the finest tack makers in the world."

"I don't want to build a house, I want to build a better saddle," I retorted.

He chuckled as he climbed onto his own horse. "Tack is the equipment used for horses."

I winced. "I knew that." Another internal cold chill hit me. I buried myself deeper into my cloak and shivered. "It's just this cold getting to me."

Xander's face showed more strain. He half-turned in his saddle and looked over the others in the group who were behind us. Spiros rode up to us and nodded. "All is ready, My Lord."

I glanced over at the elves. They stood at the edge of our saddled group. There wasn't a hoof among them. I nodded at the group. "What about them?"

Spiros smiled. "You needn't worry about them, My Lady. They are swifter of foot than many horses, particularly within these thick woods."

Xander tightened his grip on his reigns and his voice swept across our group. "Forward!"

We left the ruined camp at a fast trot and returned to the road. The elves waited until we passed before they set off after us. I glanced over my shoulder. I didn't need to. Half the columns had caught up on our right side and the other half was on our left, and they stayed there. The muddy path wasn't wide enough to accommodate horse and elf, so they flitted through the trees like ghosts, but always staying in their columns. The effect was like watching a dragon serpentine its way through a green river.

We kept to the road for a few miles before our elvish escort turned right into the woods. There wasn't even a path to follow, so our steeds jumped over and wound around a lot of trunks and brush. Each bump in the uneven ground jarred my aching body, and after another few miles my bones felt like a martini, shaken *and* stirred. My only consolation was the rain had stopped.

I opened my chapped lips to ask if we could stop for a breather, but a light ahead caught my attention. The trees thinned and revealed a sight took my remaining breath away.

Before us stood a huge tree. Its trunk could have fit a skyscraper, and its huge canopy reached as high as one. The branches were as thick as cars and the broad leaves unfurled to the size of umbrellas. Not the small, cheap ones, but the ones that could fit two or three people, if they liked each other.

Its thick branches overshadowed the mounds that lay at its trunk. Countless upheavals with its roots had created countless small hills that dotted the landscape for miles around, and within those miles was a large, emerald-hued city. Green pathways separated wood-built round houses with moss-covered roofs. Miniature versions of the large tree dotted the roads. The streets were paved with stones and traveled from hill to hill connecting the separate mounds into one big city.

At the top of the hills nestled against the trunk was a stone castle. Two towers stood at either corner along the wall that was farthest from the trunk. The walls along the sides traveled to the trunk and appeared to disappear into the smooth bark. A stone archway was the only entrance other than flying in to a courtyard. Color glass windows looked out on the city.

The boundaries of the metropolis were defined by a twenty-foot tall stone wall, but the borders were ill-equipped for defense. Many parts of the wall had collapsed, and others were so covered in green vines they could have been mistaken for a small hill. However, there was evidence of recent repairs with fresh rocks in some former holes and stained rocks where vines had been removed. Male elves with bows and quivers paced the walls.

The elven men stiffened when they saw our group approach one of the four gates that stood at the cardinal directions. At least, I think they did, but I get lost in closets.

Prince Durion hailed the guards above the gate. The elves bowed their heads, and we were allowed through the massive stone archway. It was like traveling under a bridge and into a world that perfectly combined nature and civilization. Vines grew up the walls of stone houses and twined around the chimneys. Small bits of grass grew between the rocks that made up the roads.

Many of the houses were several floors. I looked up at the windows. A few children looked out one until their mother pulled them back and shut the shutters. No one walked along the paths and there were only a few horsemen along the roads. Their armor told me they weren't civilians.

We wound our way up the hill to the castle. The gates were opened, but there was a heavy presence of guards on the parapet. We trotted into the courtyard. The ground floors on either side of us had open, arched corridors that stopped at the trunk. Set into the trunk in the center of the far wall was a pair of wooden doors guarded by two elven soldiers. Above the doors, notched into the tree and stretch up nearly out of sight, were tall, narrow windows with colorful glass in their frames. Even in the dim light of night I could see the glass reflect the tiniest amount of light and throw it back on the courtyard in a dazzling display of color.

The elves stopped in front of us and we dismounted, or rather, I slid down off my stead and dropped like a sack of potatoes onto the ground. Xander and Durion hurried over to me, and my dragon lord gathered me in his arms.

"I can stand!" I meekly insisted. In truth, my body ached with fever and I felt like a bomb had gone off in my head without release out my ears.

"And you will, but after a rest," he told me.

Durion gestured to the left side of the castle. "Your entourage may stay there, but I fear your Maiden is in need of our healers."

I eyed our host with suspicion. "There better not be any blood-drawing."

Durion bowed his head. "Nothing so barbaric, Lady Ferus."

I blinked at him. I'd never heard a last name given Xander. Heck, people rarely used his first name.

Xander frowned at Durion. "If you would dispense with the formalities and take us to the healers." He looked over his shoulder at our group.

Spiros stepped forward and bowed. "We will await your return, My Lord."

"That will be shortly. Prepare our chambers." In the background Darda bowed her head. Xander returned his attention to Durion and nodded his head. "Please lead us."

Durion guided us over to the pair of doors. The elven soldiers stepped to the side and bowed as they opened the entrance. We strode inside and into a different world.

The trunk of the tree had a hollow ring twenty feet wide and as tall. In the inner core were more doors, four total in the cardinal directions again, and more guards. The dozens of soldiers were stationed around the perimeter of the hollow area and stood at attention with long lances in one of their hands.

Durion led us around the circular hollow to the western door which we entered. The room we walked into was the size of a small auditorium and rose up only ten feet. From the ceiling hung pots, pans, glass bottles, a few knives, and the occasional dead chicken. On the floor were scattered tables filled with vials, mortars filled with stinky herbs, and enough books to fill a small public library. Half the walls were covered in bookcases, and the other half had astronomical charts and maps with red marks dotting all over. One of the maps I recognized as the one of the dragon world. Another looked like a close-up view of the Viridi Silva. I noticed there were no red dots in a large area to the northeast of the city.

Overall, the scene didn't give me faith in the skills of their healers. As though my thoughts beckoned them, two balding heads peeked out from the opposite corners of the room behind the crowded tables. They were a pair of old men with thin, curious faces. Their keen eyes swept over us before they settled on Durion. They both scurried forward, tripping over much of their mess, and stopped to bow before Durion.

"Prince Durion," they greeted him.

He smiled and bowed to them. "Greetings to you, as well, Alyan and Utiradien. I bring you good tidings."

They whipped their heads up to stare at him.

"More spice from the northern mountains, Prince?"

"Or perhaps a bear claw from the Bay?" another asked.

Durion shook his head. "No, one in need of your service." He swept his arm over Xander and me.

The eyes of the elves lit up. "A dragon patient!"

"And a lordly one!"

They would have scurried up to Xander had Durion not stepped in front of them. "A moment, my friends. The patient is the human female in his arms. She has a bad fever."

Their shoulders drooped and their faces fell.

"I see."

"We shall do what we can."

"You will be rewarded with Royal Wheat from the plains," Xander spoke up.

That perked up the two healers.

"Royal wheat?"

"A bushel of it?"

"A bushel and a half," Xander promised them.

The healers jumped at the chance for this strange wheat, and jumped at me. They both swept me from Xander's arms and hurried me over to a crowded chair. I was given to one while the other knocked aside the stack of books and dust. They set me on the hard seat and pulled away my blankets and coat with all the gentleness of a five year old opening Christmas presents.

I grabbed my shirt to keep it on me and glared at Durion. "Are you sure these guys aren't quacks?"

Durion blinked at me. "I am unfamiliar with that word, but I assure you they are very knowledgeable in illnesses."

"What about bedside manners?" I retorted as they plucked at my skin and lifted my arms.

"You are in a chair," one of them pointed out.

Xander glanced at Durion while I was harassed by my doctors. "I noticed the streets were very empty. Is there a threat to the city?"

A shadow cast itself over Durion's face as he pursed his lips. "We do not know."

The dragon lord arched an eyebrow. "You do not know, and yet the guards have been brought to the walls?"

The prince cast his eyes to the floor and furrowed his brow. "It is difficult to explain to one who is not Fae. We are the woods, and the woods are us, and when there is a disturbance we can feel it stir inside of us."

"And what do your ancient bones feel now?" Xander asked him.

Durion lifted his head and looked Xander in the eyes. "They are telling us there is a great evil coming, one we may not be able to stop."

# CHAPTER 6

"Ow!" The yelp came from me. The source of the consternation were the two elves who poked and prodded me with their smooth, long fingers. I jerked my arm away and glared at one of them. "Mind the hardware. You guys act like you've never seen a human."

"Other than travelers, humans are a rare sight in our forest and even more rare in our city," Durion explained to me. He nodded at Xander. "And in such dire times, if not for Lord Ferus-"

"I am Xander to you, Prince Durion," Xander insisted.

Durion smiled and bowed his head. "And I am Durion to you, if you would do me the honor, but for your vouching we would not have allowed anyone to travel to the city."

"When did this evil come to the forest? It was not so dire when Cayden and I passed through three months before on our way to High Castle," Xander pointed out.

Durion's shoulders fell and he sighed. "My father fell ill six months ago, and since that time the woods have grown darker."

"It was a very bad curse," Alyan spoke up.

"Very bad," Utiradien agreed.

Xander's eyes widened and flickered to the prince. "Who cast the curse?"

Durion shook his head. "We do not know."

"It was an attack on his dreams," Utiradien added.

Alyan glared at him. "No, his nightmares."

"Dreams."

"Nightmares."

Durion cleared his throat. The two quacks glared at each other and took out their fury on me with more banging and bending of my joints.

The prince turned to Xander. "Now the animals flee before the shadows, and many have left the forest entirely. There is now very little trade that dares travel along the road. Even the Sus have avoided our forest, and we are running short on the metals supplied by the mountains."

"Has there been no attempt to locate the source of this darkness?" Xander asked him.

Durion closed his eyes and shook his head. "I have suggested such an expedition, but my father will not listen. He fears it would drain our resources."

Xander smiled. "Then may I offer my resources for such a task?"

Durion pursed his lips. "I cannot ask such a favor of you, particularly since you protect your Maidens on your way home after such a long absence."

"I would never forgive myself if I did not stop to give lend my aid to a friend," Xander insisted.

The prince's face brightened. "Then we will see if my father is out of counsel, and tell him of your offer."

They turned toward the door. I tried to jump up, but the evil elves held me down to the seat, so I had to be content with stretching out my hand to my dragon lord. "Hey! What about me?"

Xander paused and looked over his shoulder. There was a mischievous smile on his lips. "You wish to leave the caring hands of Alyan and Utiradien before they have treated you?"

I glared up at the double trouble. "They've treated me to a lot of stuff already."

"Some rest will do you good, and we shall return shortly," Xander assured me.

They stepped out of the room, leaving me with the diabolical duo. The pair paused in front of me and faced me, their brows furrowed.

"Very curious," Alyan commented.

Utiradien nodded his head. "Yes, very curious indeed."

Alyan glared at his comrade. "Do you even know to what I allude?"

Utiradien returned the glare with one of his own. "Of course I do! You wonder, as do I, how this human has such an aura, do you not?"

Alyan's eyes lit up and he nodded his head. "Yes

A sneeze from me interrupted their back-and-forth. I rubbed my finger across my nostrils and frowned. "Mind letting the patient in on this diagnosis, docs? And what's this about an 'aura?'"

Alyan bowed his head to me. "Forgive us, Maiden, but I will try to explain. All living things-"

"And mountains," Utiradien added.

Alyan's eyes flickered to his friend and he frowned. "Mountains are living."

"They are not."

"We have had this discussion before. Mountains grow and die like a mighty tree."

Utiradien turned away from Alyan and crossed his arms. "I still say mountains are not living."

Alyan rolled his eyes and returned his attention to me. "All things have an aura around them. It denotes to what they belong. Green for we Arbor Fae, blue for the Mare Fae, brown for the Mons Fae and-"

"Yellow for the Rus Fae," Utiradien finished.

Alyan's face fell. He straightened and turned to Utiradien. "Would you care to explain them to the fair Maiden?"

Utiradien grinned and stepped to the forefront, bumping his companion out of the prime spot in front of me. "I would be delighted." He cleared his throat. "The aura of the Fae represent the aura colors of the areas they inhabit. All things take on such auras to varying degrees, even humans and Sus, but we Fae are the brightest."

"You are not getting to the point!" Alyan scolded him.

Utiradien looked over his shoulder. "Patience!"

I raised my stiff-jointed hand. My body felt even worse after all of their 'healing.' "So what color am I?"

Utiradien opened his mouth, paused, and shut his jaws before he looked back to his compatriot. "Blue?"

Alyan nodded. "Blue."

Utiradien returned his attention to me. "Blue."

I shrugged. "And that means what?"

"It means you have lived your whole life in water," Alyan told me.

I raised an eyebrow. "*In* water?" They both nodded. I shook my head. "I hate to break it to you, fellas, but I haven't even lived *near* water any time in my life except that time when the pipes in my apartment broke. That was a flood that would have made Noah jealous."

Utiradien's eyes lit up and a smile spread across his face. "Noah! Yes! He would be what you are."

I blinked at him. "Come again?"

Alyan scurried to the front. "What my confused colleague is trying to say is Noah is your ancestor."

I arched an eyebrow. "*The* Noah? Flood and everything?" They both nodded. I shook my head. "You're kidding right?"

"You are of the Mare Fae, thus he is your ancestor," Alyan insisted.

"I'm a *what*?"

"A water fae," Utiradien clarified.

I pointed at myself. "I'm an elf?"

They both wrinkled their noses. "We prefer the term fae," Alyan told me.

"Elves are those in foolish stories meant for children," Utiradien added.

I shook my head. "I think you guys have been sniffing too many herbs. I'm just a human."

The pair of 'fae' hovered over me with dark shadows over their angered faces. "You doubt our judgment?" Alyan questioned me.

"You dare suggest we do not know what our own skills tell us?" Utiradien chimed in.

I shrank beneath their glares and held up my hands. "Easy there, guys, I'm just saying there's got to be a mistake. I'm a nobody."

Alyan leaned away and scoffed. "A Maiden is not a nobody."

Utiradien bobbed his head up and down. "A Maiden is a special human, a fae of your world."

I stared at them with a raised eyebrow and troubled eyes. They stared at me with wide, eager smiles. I stood up.

"I'm leaving."

Their faces showed their dismay and I was promptly pulled back onto the chair.

"No!"

"You must stay!"

I glared up at them as they stepped back. "You two are quacks. I'm not a fae, elf, fairy, or even a goblin, no matter what some guys have told me. Besides, you haven't even cured me of this stupid cold."

"We will cure you this moment!" Alyan assured me.

"And I will fetch the cure!" Utiradien offered. He scurried into the far reaches of the room and rummaged through the mess. Dried twigs and books flew over his back, and a cloud of dust floated over and concealed his efforts.

Alyan's voice caught my attention away from the disaster area. "Why do you doubt our word?"

I looked back to him and snorted. "I told you, I'm not that special."

A soft smile slipped onto his lips. "Your modesty is admirable, but in this instance it does you no justice."

"It's not modesty, it's-"

"The cure!" Utiradien shouted.

He hurried from his dust cloud and over to us. In one hand he held a vial of green juice and in the other was a sprig of some tree. He beamed with glee as he held them both out to Alyan.

Alyan arched an eyebrow and nodded at the sprig. "Why did you bring the selva sprig?"

"For good measure," Utiradien explained.

Alyan sighed and shook his head. "The selva sprig is only used to ward off unnatural evil. It does nothing against a natural illness."

Utiradien's face drooped. "Oh, well, never mind then." He tossed the sprig over his shoulder and popped the cork of the vial. A scent of fresh grass mixed with manure came to my nostrils. "But I am certain this is the voide for colds."

I leaned away from the vial and eyed the pair. "Are you two sure you're elves?"

Alyan smiled as he took the vial from his compatriot. "We are fae, and we are here to help."

I swallowed as they approached me. It was two against one, and I really was starting to feel like the shitty smell coming from that bottle. I held up one hand. They stopped.

I held out my hand. "I'll take it myself."

The two almost looked disappointed, but Alyan handed me the vial. I held my breath, stiffened my jaw, and downed the small container. The flavor was a mix of freshly cut grass and day-old farts. It was the type of food someone would pay a lot of money to eat once just to say that they did.

I glared at the pair. "Did you two get this stuff out of-" I paused. My feverish head cleared like the parting of clouds. All my aches and pains vanished. I felt ten years younger, and looked down at myself just to make sure I wasn't reverting back to those terrible teen years. Nope, everything was still there. I raised the empty vial and studied the meager remains of the contents. "What's in this stuff?"

Alyan took the vial back. "You would not wish to know."

I shuddered and stood. "So can I leave now?"

The fae stepped aside and both gestured to the door. They bowed their heads. "We are ever at your service, Maiden of the Fae."

I scurried past them, but turned and bowed at the waist in response as I walked backward to the door. "Um, likewise."

I slipped out of there before they took me up on my offer.

# CHAPTER 7

I stepped out into the hall and shut the door behind me. The wood clanged shut and I winced as the noise echoed around the hollow hall. The guards didn't even flinch. I looked left and right. There was no sign of Xander or Durion.

I cautiously walked up to one of the imposing, unsmiling guards. "You don't happen to know where the prince and dragon lord went, do you?"

The guard didn't look at me as he replied. "To the southern door."

I saluted and stepped backward away from him. "Thanks." He didn't return the gesture, or any other, for that matter.

I hurried to the south which I guessed was the one near the double-door entrance. The door was shut, but a shut door never stopped a determined girl. I opened it a crack and peeked inside. A wide, winding staircase stared back at me. The steps were long enough to fit the marching fae who escorted us to this scared city. Small alcoves in either wall held glass jars with floating lights that lit the way.

Echoing voices floated down to me. I slipped inside and shut the door behind me before I tiptoed up the steps.

I should have run. The staircase wound its way up so long that by the time I reached the top I felt like a corkscrew. There hadn't been a single break until the top where a landing of some ten feet led to a pair of large, wooden doors. Intricate scenes of hunting, fishing and feasting were carved into the dark, weathered wood.

One of the doors was slightly ajar. I slipped over and leaned my head close to the carvings. It gave me a great view of the carved figures. I was surprised to see they didn't have pointed ears.

"Your kind offer of assistance is appreciated, Lord of Alexandria, but we have no need of your men," an ancient male voice spoke up.

I peeked through the opening. The doors led to a large throne room replete with fae decked out in colorful robes of green and brown. A thrown of vines sat against the wall opposite the doors, and seated on the throne was an old fae with a laurel crown on his head. His face was stern as he looked down at Xander and Durion who stood before him.

Durion stepped forward. "But Father, we cannot stand idly by while the darkness invades the forest!"

One of the taller fae beside the throne bristled at him. "We do not 'do nothing,' as you say, Prince Durion. The walls are being rebuilt as we speak, and our guards are at the ready for any attack."

Durion glared at him. "It would be better if we met the fight at a place other than the city."

The tall fae gestured to the room with both hands. "But which way is the threat, Prince Durion? Where shall we meet this faceless and placeless enemy?"

"I mean to find the answers to your questions with this expedition," Durion insisted.

The old kingly fae held up his hand and the room silenced. He closed his eyes and shook his head. "There will be no more talk of this. I will not allow such a foolhardy expedition, and I forbid you or anyone from taking part in such a waste of resources. Have I made myself-"

"Eep!"

I was so focused on the conversation that I didn't realize how hard I leaned against the entrance. Faced with the prospect of supporting my weight, the door swung inward and I toppled into the room. I rolled head-over-heels a couple of times and came to a stop on my rear. The guards came to a stop around me with their pointed spears pointed at my throat.

I stretched my neck and tried not to swallow as a shaky smile slipped onto my lips. "H-hiya."

"Miriam!" Xander scolded me.

"I thought I'd just drop by for a spell," I told him.

The king leapt to his feet and the soldiers around me pressed their points against my flesh. "Who is this woman and to what spell does she refer?"

I snorted. "It's only a figure of speech."

The thin fae beside the throne sneered at me. "Watch your tongue! You stand before Thorontur, king of Metsan Keskella and lord of all of Virea Metsa!"

Xander knelt on one knee before the king and bowed his head. "I apologize for this intrusion, Your Highness. She is my Maiden who has apparently followed me to your counsel room."

The king pursed his lips, but his eyes flickered to the guards and he gave a curt nod. They withdrew their weapons and I could breathe again.

Xander stood and strode over to me. He helped me climb to my shaky feet. "Sorry..." I whispered.

He shook his head. His eyes were troubled. "There is little to apologize for. Your entrance came at the end of our interview." He glanced over his shoulder at the high court of the fae and he bowed his head. "If you will excuse us, Your Highness, we will take our leave."

The king resumed his seat and returned the bow. Xander led me from the throne room and down the stairs.

"So I'm guessing things didn't go so well for you guys?" I commented.

He nodded. "Unfortunately, yes. The king is so full of fear he will not be reasoned with."

"Does he even know what he's afraid of?" I wondered.

We reached the bottom of the stairs and stopped at the landing between the last step and the door. Xander glanced back up the stairs and furrowed his brow. "I believe he knows more than he allows his subjects, and even his own son, to know."

"So what now?"

He returned his attention to me and the corners of his lips curled up in a soft smile. "The healers did their task well. You are in fine spirits."

My eyebrows crashed down and I poked a finger into his chest. "Speaking of that, you left me alone with a bunch of quacks."

He chuckled. "I do not understand your meaning, but your tone is as clear a truth as ever I heard."

I crossed my arms and glared at him. "It's because I don't like to sugarcoat anything."

"I will remember-" He paused and glanced up the stairs. A shadow traveled down the wall, and in a moment the prince appeared.

He stopped beside us and bowed to Xander. "I must apologize for my father's behavior. He is normally not so short-tempered, nor so-"

"Paranoid?" I suggested.

Durion pursed his lips and nodded. "I fear so."

"What will you do now that His Highness has disallowed your venture?" Xander asked him.

Durion glanced past us at the door and then over his shoulder at the stairs. He met Xander's eyes and lowered his voice to a whisper. "Will you meet me at the Hemlock Inn in an hour? There is something I wish to discuss with you."

Xander nodded. "I will come."

Durion smiled. "Good. If you will excuse me." He slipped past us and out the door.

I looked to Xander and arched an eyebrow. "What are you two planning?"

He shook his head. "We will know within the hour, but for now let us return to our friends. They are no doubt anxious to see us."

Xander led me through the doors and out into the courtyard. Cayden, Stephanie, and Spiros stood behind the columns in the left patio and straightened when we exited the tree. They strode over to us.

"What news?" Cayden asked him.

Xander pursed his lips as he looked over their curious faces. "Dire news. It seems our friends are in great need of our help against an unknown foe."

Spiros clasped the hilt of his sword. "Our hands are ever at the ready for the call, My Lord."

The dragon lord smiled. "I have no doubt of that, but regardless of their need they have refused our help."

Spiros furrowed his brow. "Then they wish to fight alone?"

Xander shook his head. "They do not wish to fight at all, but to barricade themselves in their city and hope the darkness passes over them."

"Won't it?" Cayden spoke up. He gestured around to the great city. "This city has stood for a thousand years without being taken. What force in these realms can match their strength and overcome it?"

"That is what we must find out and I believe their prince hopes to do the same, but we shall meet him and discuss matters more thoroughly in an hour," Xander told them. He turned to me and smiled. "In the meanwhile, I believe two Maidens may wish to see what the city of the Arbor Fae has to offer."

I snorted. "I'd just like to know what this place is called."

"The name of this city is Metsan Keskella, and it lies in the heart of Virea Metsa," Cayden told me.

I raised an eyebrow at Xander. "You told me the forest's name was Viridi Silva."

"Not all people speak the same tongue in our world, nor do they settle on the same name. In both the language of the realms and the fae the name of the forest means 'green forest,'" he told me.

Stephanie swept her eyes over the greenery around us and smiled. "It's very beautiful, isn't it?"

Xander offered me his arm as a hint of sunlight peeked over the trees in the east. Our long night was nearly over. "And awaiting both your inspections, My Ladies."

I accepted his arm while Stephanie took Cayden's. Xander glanced over his shoulder at Spiros. "We are unfortunately short on Maidens, Captain."

Spiros grinned. "My lady is your orders, My Lord, but I hope she will not be too demanding."

"Then they are to prepare half the soldiers to be around the area of the Hemlock Inn. The other half are to remain around the rooms," Xander told him.

Spiros bowed his head. "It will be done."

"Then let us be off."

# CHAPTER 8

Xander and Cayden led us on a guided tour through the winding, grassy streets of the green city. There were ivy-covered walls and large, blooming flowers to admire, and beautifully carved doors to study. The sights would have been more enjoyable if there were more people, but the place was a ghost town. Shadows peeked out of the windows and soldiers moved to and fro, but otherwise the streets were deserted.

That is, until we walked down one of the dozen hills to a small square. I heard the laughter of children and the way opened into the cobblestone area. A gurgling, three-tiered stone fountain stood in the center. Its crystal-clear water grew lily-pads on its surface, and one could lean over the wide wall of the bottom pond to brush their fingers against the light pink flowers.

Seated atop the wide wall was a familiar character. It was a pig-man like Blake and his cohorts. The man wore tan leather jeans and a shirt under a heavy leather coat that reached to his ankles. Black boots covered his cloven feet, and over one shoulder and across his body was a strap from which dangled a large satchel. His blond hair was in stark contrast to his tanned skin, and one of his tusks that peeked out from his bottom lip was broken.

What surprised me the most was the crowd around him. A half dozen fae kids stood in front of him. Their heads were tilted back and their eyes were on his upraised hand that he held above his head. A mischievous grin lay on his lips as he waved his closed fist.

"Come on, you kids can do better than that," he teased them.

"It's a phoenix!" a small boy yelled.

"Ith's a bird!" a little girl lisped.

The boy glared at her. "He already said it wasn't a bird."

She glared back at him. "But you said ith was a phoenix."

"That's because a phoenix is a special bird," he countered.

The pig-man chuckled. "It isn't any type of bird, special or not, but you'd better keep guessing or this treasure's going to fly away."

"But you said it wasn't a bird!" the boy pointed out.

"And it's not, but birds aren't the only fliers," the man argued. He glanced in our direction. A twinkle slipped into his eyes. "Well, well, it looks like my pet's already escaped."

The kids turned to us. One of the older ones squinted at us and frowned. "It's just a bunch of dragons."

# REALMS OF THE DRAGONS

"We have ourselves a winner!" the pig-man exclaimed.

He lowered his hand and opened his palm. There, nestled in his pudgy hand, was a small dragon carved from polished stone. He handed the dragon to the boy, and the others crowded around their fortunate friend to admire his treasure.

"Wow. . ." the boy breathed.

The pig-man chuckled and ruffled the boy's hair. "Take good care of him or he's liable to fly off."

A smile spread across his lips. "I'm going to show Mother!"

He raced across the square with the others behind him eager for another glimpse of the prize. The pig-man stood as Xander and Cayden led us over to him. He smiled and bowed low at the waist to us. "An early good morning to you, My Lords," he greeted us.

Xander and Cayden bowed their heads. Stephanie mimicked the movement, but I glared at the pig-man.

"What brings such illustrious lords to a city of the fae?" the man asked us.

"The woods, or rather the darkness that spreads over them," Xander replied.

The pig-man nodded. "It's a pain to have an enemy you don't know about, but-" he slipped close to Xander and lowered his voice as his eyes flickered over the empty square, "-there are rumors the king knows who it is."

"Are these rumors reliable?" Xander wondered.

The man pulled back and feigned a gasp. "My Lord, would I lie to you?"

"Yes," I spoke up.

He paused and swept his eyes over Stephanie and me. "Where are my manners? You haven't introduced me to these lovely creatures with you." He winked at the men. "New servants for My Lords?"

"Our Maidens," Cayden corrected him.

The pig-man straightened and coughed into his fist. "I see. Well, my apologies if I came off as rude. I've been traveling so much lately I forgot that was taking place." He looked at us and nodded. "Yes, quite fine specimens this time."

"You would know. . ." I muttered.

He raised an eyebrow and pressed a finger against his chest. "*I* would know, My Lady?"

Xander chuckled. "My Maiden has mistaken you for a companion of Blake."

The pig-man straightened to his full short height and his flat nose wrinkled. "That swine? I know his family has done you dragon lords a great service fetching the Maidens all these years, but I wouldn't bet my last bronze coin on his honesty, or even my first one."

I raised an eyebrow. "So what do you do?"

"I'm a Sus of a different color, My Lady," he assured me. He swept into a bow and lowered his head. "My name is Tillit, My Lady, and it means 'trust,' for there's no better Sus in the world to trust than Tillit."

"Then these rumors are true?" Xander challenged him.

Tillit nodded. "Aye, My Lord, as true as the nose on my face. Besides, my nose can smell it." He narrowed his eyes and flickered them over the area. "Something's going on around here that isn't normal. It's like a spell's been cast and everyone's waiting around to see what it does."

Xander rummaged through his coat and pulled out a small leather bag with a drawstring top. He held out the bag to the Sus. "We require your help in procuring more information, particularly what the king may know."

Tillit took the bag and bowed his head. "I am ever at your humble command, My Lord."

Xander chuckled. "Only so long as my coins hold out."

"And that, as well, My Lord," Tillit agreed as he pocketed the bag inside his shirt. "But you've purchased for yourself the best Sus in the world, and I promise I won't fail you."

"Always the same with your humility?" Xander teased.

"Humility is an emotion that doesn't pay, My Lord," Tillit replied. "If I start saying I'm only one of tens of thousands of other Sus then how will I get any business?"

"He has wisdom," Cayden spoke up.

Tillit smiled at the young dragon lord and bowed his head. "A compliment from the Dragon of the Plains is much appreciated."

Cayden started back. "How do you know who I am?"

Tillit raised his hand and winked. "Tillit knows much, and tells less than he knows except when the price is right."

"Is my price adequate to hurry you on my task?" Xander reminded him.

Tillit straightened and saluted the dragon lord. "At once, My Lord! I shall not dawdle any longer!" He scurried past us and disappeared into one of the side streets.

Cayden turned to Xander. "What an odd character. Where did you meet him before?"

"Tillit was one of my father's most faithful friends, and my mother was very fond of him," Xander revealed.

I furrowed my brow as I studied him. "Hasn't your mom been gone a long time?"

He nodded. "Nearly fifty years."

I jerked my head in the direction where the Sus had gone. "But that guy didn't look over forty."

"Many creatures in our world have lifespans that may seem prodigious to you, but are very commonplace here," he explained. He looked up at the sky. "But we had best set our feet to the inn. Durion awaits us."

# CHAPTER 9

We traveled through the maze of streets to the commercial hill. Open shops, smithies, and taverns crowded together for space and customers. I counted a half dozen pubs along a single street.

"Do the fae drink that much?" I asked our dragon guides.

Xander smiled while Cayden nodded. "They drink to celebrate their festivals and honor their gods and patrons."

I nodded at the street with its few fae. "So how come I don't see anybody staggering around? Too early?"

"Their bodies have a high immunity to intoxication, and it is considered an honor to be able to drink as much as any fae," he explained.

"So are all the fae like that? I mean, all the different types?" I wondered.

Xander arched an eyebrow. "How did you learn that?"

I leaned toward him and glared at the dragon lord. "A certain someone left me with two crazy fae, remember?"

"But you are cured," he pointed out.

I crossed my arms and shrank into myself as we walked down the hill. "You'd better hope insanity isn't contagious. . ."

Xander stopped us at a small establishment. Above the door was a wooden sign, but I couldn't read the unfamiliar letters. I could make out a carving of a plant over the words. Here was the Hemlock Inn.

At that moment I recalled another of our crew who we were supposed to meet there. A quick glance around didn't tell me anything. "Where's Spiros?"

Xander's crooked smile slipped onto his handsome face. "We needn't wait for him. He will be forthcoming soon enough."

We slipped into the inn and found ourselves in a shadowed pub. Little alcoves in the walls to our left were fitted with the same glowing glass balls. The round tables in the center of the floor likewise had the illuminated glass. At the far corner was the bar and a staircase that led to the advertised 'inn' part of the business. A few patrons were seated at the tables with their drinks cradled in their hands.

One of them beckoned to us from the darkest corner, and we joined Durion at his table. He was barely recognizable in a plain gray cloak with a hood that covered his face.

Durion's eyes flickered over us as he spoke in a low voice. "I feel I must apologize for my outfit, but I was followed from the palace. Fortunately, I managed to elude my pursuers."

"The palace soldiers?" Xander asked him.

Durion pursed his lips and shook his head. "No, several of my father's personal guards. He means to keep me from leaving the city." He balled a hand into a fist and clenched his teeth. "But I cannot wait for this darkness to swallow my people and my city."

My dragon lord smiled. "My men and I are still yours to command."

"As are mine," Cayden spoke up.

The prince bowed his head. "And I will be grateful for-" The door to the inn opened and shadows stretched across the floor.

A group of armor-clad soldiers stepped inside and looked over the room. It didn't take them long to find us huddled in the corner. They marched through the tables, frightening several of the patrons away from their drinks, and stopped at ours.

The leader bowed to Durion. "My Prince, I must ask you to return to the palace with us."

Durion frowned. "For what reason?"

The guard raised his head. "Your father wishes to speak with you."

Durion gestured to us. "You may tell the king that I am entertaining our guests, and will be with him as soon as possible."

The guard grasped the hilt of his sword. "I apologize, My Prince, but I was given clear instructions that you were to come with us without delay."

"He is not finished with My Lord."

The voice came from behind the guards. One of the nearby patrons stood from his table and threw aside the worn cap to reveal himself as Spiros. The other half dozen patrons who remained stood with him and showed themselves as soldiers of both Cayden and Xander.

The fae leader curled his lips back in a sneer. "You would dare attack the royal guards?"

Spiros unsheathed his sword and pointed the blade at them. "I would not dare attack you, but if you insist-"

They insisted, and a brawl broke out between dragon and fae. The close-proximity meant most of the support soldiers couldn't use their long spears on each other, so they were left to beat each other with fists and the butt-ends of their swords, if they had them.

Xander shoved Stephanie and me into a corner as the battle ensued. He, Cayden and Durion duked it out with the guards. I watched one of Xander's long punches bend the metal plate of one of the lower-level guards.

Xander stumbled back and flexed his fingers as he looked out over the carnage. Ruined chairs and tables littered the floor. The walls were punctuated by deep indents, and more than one combatant was on the ground wrestling with their foe.

"Do no harm to them!" Xander commanded our soldiers.

Spiros shoved his opponent away with his shoulder and blocked a punch from another one. "These fine fae make your request a most difficult one, My Lord!"

Xander punched one in the cheek. The fae spun around and fell face-first onto the floor. He didn't get up. "Imagine they are me in our practice bouts!"

His captain conked a fae on the top of the head with the hilt of his sword. "I cannot, My Lord! These opponents would be far easier to defeat!"

Our fun little tussle was interrupted when the door swung open. The cavalry had arrived, but it wasn't ours. More fae soldiers crowded the doorway. Cayden and Spiros shoved their shoulders against the wood and slammed the door in the faces of the second wave of fae.

"Through the back!" Durion shouted.

Most of the first wave was either unconscious or on the losing end of their fight. Xander and Cayden's young soldier from the camp shoved the broken furniture against the front door, pinning the wood shut on its own. I grabbed Stephanie and together we stumbled across the broken floor to the bar. A hallway to its left led to the rear of the building and another entrance.

The rear door brought us out on a narrow, cobblestone alley. Even their alleys were clean. Durion hurried to the forefront of our group and gestured to the way ahead of him. "This way!"

We rushed through the maze of narrow alleys that zigged and zagged up and down the many hilly districts of the city. Our path brought us to the northern gate of the green metropolis. A half dozen guards met us at the shut gate.

"Open the gates! Quickly!" Durion shouted.

"Wait!" came a call behind us.

I looked over my shoulder to see a contingency of guards in hot pursuit. Fortunately, the soldiers at the entrance were obedient to a fault. They opened the gate on instinct and we sprinted through into the thick forest.

Our followers stopped at the gate. My last look of them as we disappeared into the trees told me they weren't happy.

We didn't stop running until we were well away from the walls of the city. By that time my legs felt like they wanted to fall off, and I was thinking about letting them. Our resting place was a wide spot in the dense forest. Stephanie and I collapsed on a soft, moss-covered log as the men in armor stood at attention in front of us. The dragons and fae were barely winded, or they were just acting cool.

"I feel I have done a great injustice to you in allowing you to come with me," Durion spoke up.

Xander turned to our resident fae and shook his head. "This world of ours is connected. We would not have left you alone to face this great darkness that will surely encroach on our own lands."

"But my father-"

"Will forgive us, but only if we succeed in routing this darkness from the forest," Xander pointed out.

Spiros moved to stand behind Xander's shoulder and looked around. "My Lord, the birds." The group quieted and looked around.

I tilted my head to one side and listened. "I don't hear anything."

Xander pursed his lips and nodded. "That is the what concerns us. There are no birds here." He returned his attention to Durion. "What was your plan in leading us out the northern gate? I believe it has not been used in many years."

Durion nodded. "That is true, but I believe the answers to our questions lies in this direction. My father holds a tight rule over all the Virea Metsa but for a small patch of northern territory. It is forbidden for anyone to go there, but I believe that is where we must travel."

"Why is it forbidden?" Cayden spoke up.

Durion shook his head. "I do not know. The reason has passed out of the memory of all who now live, but I do know the decree is many thousands of years old, long before you dragons rose up to become lords of the plains."

"Then we shall start there with our search," Xander agreed. "Lead us."

# CHAPTER 10

I tried to stand, but my legs were shaky. Stephanie, too, winced as she stood. I raised my hand. "Could we humans have just ten more minutes? We're Maidens, not roadrunners."

Durion glanced back the way we came. "The risk is too great. My father may risk sending a few of his guard to retrieve us."

"Then we will compromise," Xander spoke up. He walked over to me and swept me into his arms.

I glared at him and shoved my hand with splayed fingers in his face. "Five minutes! Just give me five minutes!"

Xander turned to Durion as Stephanie was likewise placed in Cayden's grasp. "Lead on."

Durion nodded, and we marched after him into the dense forest. The western path to the city had been rocky, but this way was almost suicidal. Fallen trees the size of semis littered the forest floor. One of the soldiers leapt onto the surface of one and the bark broke beneath his weight. He fell into the hole, but caught the lip of the bark and pulled himself out. Another walked into a web of vines that nearly strangled them but for the fast action of Durion and his sword.

I clung to Xander and watched the last hacking away of the homicidal overgrowth. "I'm starting to think maybe flying isn't such a bad idea."

"Since we do not know what we seek we may miss it beneath the forest canopy," Xander pointed out.

I looked to him. "But don't you dragon guys have a aerial map of this area or something like that?"

He shook his head. "Our maps are not so precise, nor so complete. Our world is vast with many separate kingdoms. We respect each kingdom's territory, even if it means avoiding their skies."

"So what you're saying is you don't have a map of this place."

"That is correct."

I sighed and sank deeper into his arms. "Perfect. . ."

"The forbidden territory is very small, My Lady, if that gives you some comfort," Durion told me as he flung aside the last of the vines.

I looked around us at the dark shadows of the tall trees. A chill sank into my bones and made me shudder. "I hope it's not too far. This place gives me the creeps."

"It is a few more miles, more than the distance we have traveled," he told me.

And with that cheerful bit of news we continued on our journey through the Forest of No Return, called that because

I would never have found my way back. There weren't any paths, not even those made by animals, and the canopy was so thick only a few beams of sunlight filtered through to the forest floor. The farther we went, the colder the damp on my bones became until I felt as cold as I had after my unscheduled swim.

We traveled through the darkness for several more hours, and I was glad when I spotted an opening in the trees ahead of us. Durion, however, slowed our march and held up his hand to stop us.

I couldn't stop a whimper that slipped from my lips. The air around us was like breathing through a hot mask. My body felt squeezed by some invisible hands.

Xander looked down at me with a furrowed brow. In such a heavy atmosphere words were forbidden. I pointed at the clearing up ahead. He shook his head.

Durion glanced over his shoulder to look at us. He spoke in a hushed whisper. "There is something amiss here. It would be best if your men remained behind us and touched nothing."

Xander swept his eyes over the guards. They nodded in understanding. Durion crept ahead and we followed.

My initial joy at seeing the clearing was soon turned to disgust. The closer we came to the area the more putrid the air became. I slapped my hand over my mouth to stifle the awful smell.

We reached the clearing and stepped out of the trees. The mid-afternoon sun shone down on us, but none of its warmth reached to the ground. The suffocating air of the forest was replaced by a tension, like the world waited in anticipation for something to be loosed upon it.

# REALMS OF THE DRAGONS

The large meadow was devoid of trees, but it was not devoid of plants. A huge growth of vines stood in the center of the clearing and piled atop itself so it reached two hundred feet into the sky. The shadows it cast stretched across the meadow and ended just short of where we stood.

A harsh, cold breeze blew past us and ruffled the leaves on the vines. The leaves waved as us as though beckoning us closer, and beneath them I saw something strange. Stones. Large, carved blocks of shining marble and solid granite lay under the vines. They were stacked into thick, towering walls with archways and windows. One larger, ivy-covered archway revealed a large courtyard in the center of the vine mound.

What we saw before us were the ruins of a fortified castle.

Durion swept his eyes over the castle and shook his head. His voice was so low I barely caught the words. "By the gods. The stories were true."

"What stories?" Xander questioned him.

Durion shook himself and turned to us. "It is not something we wish to admit, but we fae were not always alone in these woods. Stories told for thousands of years have hinted at a kingdom of men that once stood in the northern part of the forest. They were a wild men who lived in a great stone house and feasted on the bounty the forest offered them, but they did not repay the kindness of the trees with respect. The men tore the trees down for the fires to cook their feasts. The animals fled before their arrows and the plants withered beneath their many feet. The gods themselves grew tired of their tyranny and drove them into their stone house. The house, or rather castle, was set alight by the thunder of a great storm. All inside perished, but it is said that that night was not the last of them or their evil."

Xander arched an eyebrow. "How can that be?"

He pursed his lips and returned his attention to the ruined castle. His green eyes flickered from moss-covered stone to moss-covered stone, and every moment they narrowed further and further. "The gods only punished them, they did not destroy them."

I snorted. "Killing them in a fire sounds pretty destroyed to me."

Durion walked forward and pressed his palm against the exterior wall. A faint green glow pulsed between his hand and the stones. His light reminded me of the blue light of the river fae. "Reckless malevolence is very difficult to destroy. It consumes itself and grows bitter with its poor feast. The malevolence spreads beyond its boundaries seeking other flavors."

"But why now? And why did the evil spread so quickly?" Cayden spoke up.

The prince shook his head. "I cannot fathom, but what I feel from these stones is a deep darkness that won't be appeased until it has consumed the entire forest."

"Then what must we do to destroy this thing?" Xander asked him.

Durion half-turned to us. "I might try a cleansing-" He froze and his eyes widened.

Durion whipped his head back to his arm. My gaze followed his. The soft green glow in the stone was now a red hue. The light pulsed beneath his hand and solidified into a glob of tendrils. The tendrils stretched out and latched on to Durion's arm.

I heard Stephanie gasp. Durion grabbed his glowing arm and tugged. It didn't move. The tendrils slithered up his arm toward his head.

# REALMS OF THE DRAGONS

Xander and Cayden set us down and leapt forward. My dragon lord grabbed his arm and pulled back, but it wouldn't budge. Cayden tried to tear away at the rocks, but his clawed hands did nothing but scratch the hard surface.

Durion pushed them away. "Get back! Get back!"

The dragon lords stumbled back and prepared for another assault when the speed of the red light quickened. Durion shut his eyes as it swallowed him whole. For a moment we couldn't see his body. There was only the red, pulsing light.

That light receded and revealed Durion, but he wasn't the same. His eyes had become a bright red. There was a smirk curled onto his lips that distorted his handsome features. His skin was as pale as the marble above us.

His formerly trapped arm dropped to his side and he turned to face us. When he spoke his voice echoed as though hundreds of other people were speaking at the same time. "Freedom. Sweet, joyous freedom."

Cayden took a step toward him. "Prince! Do you-" Xander grabbed his arm.

"Do not approach that thing," my dragon lord warned him.

Cayden looked over his shoulder at Xander and frowned. "What has happened to him?"

Xander looked past him at Durion. "He is possessed by the evil in the stones."

Durion, or what used to be the prince, raised his hands in front of him so the palms faced each other. A red light glowed from his left hand and a green from his right. They floated from his palms and swirled around each other like two paints being mixed in a can.

The hairs on the back of my neck stood on end. "Not good!" I shouted.

The colors spun faster and faster. They created a wind around them that swirled into a small tornado between Durion's hands. The green light was swallowed by the red, and that lone color plunged itself deep into the earth like a large drill. The ground split and cracked as the tornado dug deep into its crust.

A rumbling echoed from the depths of the earth. Dozens of cracks spread like wildfire from the bored hole to the castle behind Durion. Most traveled under the large archway and into the ruined courtyard. They stopped at random points and dug deeper into the earth. The gaps widened and beams of red light shot up toward the sky.

Skeletal hands reached out of the gaps and grasped the edges of the holes. The creatures pulled themselves into view.

They were zombies.

# CHAPTER 11

There weren't just a few zombies. Hundreds of the things dragged themselves from their fiery graves. The charred creatures-men, women and children-stared around themselves with red, glowing eyes. Their terrible moans echoed off their massive tombstone. Durion, or whatever he was now, dropped his hands to his sides and the light in front of him vanished, but the damage was done.

The zombies latched on to the vines and moss, and with every touch the plant was drained of its color. The vines turned gray and withered, and the green light from their lives entered the zombies. The green from the plants rejuvenated parts of their rotten bodies, creating flesh atop bone, but they still remained more corpse than corporeal. The creatures shuffled or crawled on all fours over to the trees and grasped the trunks. The tops of the trees lost their color first and drained down until all the life was absorbed by the zombies.

"My goddess. . ." Cayden murmured.

The zombies whipped their heads toward our group. Their hideous red eyes glowed like the coals of hell, or that time my mom caught her soup on fire. Right then I wished I was back in her kitchen watching the flames jump to the ceiling. The creatures hissed and stooped on all fours. They crawled toward us and gnashed their teeth.

Xander shifted into a defensive position and kept his eyes on the creatures as he spoke. "Prepare to fly."

One of Xander's men closest to us tightened his grip on his lance. "But My Lord-"

"We cannot win against this foe, at least not yet," my dragon lord warned him.

"You cannot escape our forest," Durion called out. He stretched his arms out on either side of him and raised them to the sky.

The forest around us groaned. The trees that made up the canopy stretched their long branches over the sky. Vines traveled up the trees and threw themselves across the gap between the tree line and the castle, creating a thick net of stalks. Their leaves and stems blocked out the sun and enveloped us in a near-total darkness. I could barely make out the tree line that stood twenty feet away.

What I could see, however, were those awful red eyes. They glowed in the dim light, and they were getting closer.

"Retreat to the city!" Xander shouted.

Our troop turned tail and ran for it. Stephanie and I were in the middle of the pack, but falling fast behind the fast strides of the dragon men before Xander scooped me into his arms. Stephanie had the same done to her by Cayden, and we were carried to the front of the lines, or what was left of them. The men abandoned the trail for any clear path. The canopy snapped shut just ahead of us, keeping the dragons from using their wings.

I glanced over Xander's shoulder. The red-eyed zombies lunged from tree trunk to tree trunk. Their path was tainted by the dead and dying trees left by their touch. They were fast, but the dragon lords and their men were faster. They leapt over large trunks and knocked away barriers with their taloned hands so that the distance between the zombies and us grew greater until I could barely see their glow.

Then catastrophe. One of our company tripped over a root and fell to the ground. His shout brought the whole company to a standstill. We turned and watched the roots of the nearby trees entwine themselves around our fallen comrades body.

"Liam!" Cayden shouted. It was one of his own soldiers who fell, and the same who helped Stephanie at the camp.

The young dragon lord left Stephanie in the care of one of his men and rushed forward to help our fallen comrade. Xander turned to the others and pointed ahead of us. "Take our Maidens and keep going! That's an order!"

"But we cannot leave you, My Lord!" Spiros insisted.

I moved away from Spiros so he couldn't snatch me up. "I'm not going anywhere!"

"I won't leave, either!" Stephanie spoke up.

"My Lord?" Spiros asked Xander.

Xander's eyes flickered to me and frowned. "Leave us and go to the city. The fae must be warned."

"But My-"

Xander shoved his captain ahead of us. "For the sake of their city, go!"

Spiros pursed his lips, but nodded. The men reluctantly abandoned their lords and fled into the woods. Xander turned to me and grabbed my shoulders. "Remain here."

I could only nod as he hurried to join Cayden. The younger dragon lord was trying desperately to cut away at the tree roots. More and more brown, slithery coils wrapped themselves around the solider.

I glanced past them. My breath stopped as I beheld the familiar glowing red eyes. I pointed at our incoming foes. "Xander!"

He lifted his head and followed my finger. Ahead of the pack of zombies was Prince. His face was now a ghoulish gray color and there was a sick, crooked grin on his ruby-red lips. He floated a half foot above the forest floor with his arms spread out on either side of him like a preacher with his cult of followers.

The soldier grabbed Cayden's upper arm with one hand and looked up into his face. "Please, My Lord, leave me! There is nothing you can do!"

Cayden shook his head. "I will not-" His soldier shoved him away.

"Grant me this last wish! Leave me!" the man insisted.

Xander grabbed Cayden's shoulder. "We cannot help him if we do not ourselves survive."

Cayden pressed his lips together, but finally nodded. "May the gods bless you."

The soldier smiled. "They will so long as you are safe, My Lord."

The dragon lords turned and rushed over to where we stood some forty feet off. I looked past him at the man as he continued to struggle to free himself from the vines and roots. The scene tugged at my heart.

I looked into Xander's eyes as he came up to me and pointed at the soldier. "We can't leave him! We just can't!"

Xander blocked my view of the man as he swept me into his arms. "We must obey his last wish."

A cry from the soldier made us turn around. The root tendrils tightened their hold on the man as the zombies and Durion caught up to him. The zombies leapt on the man and grabbed his arms and legs. There came the same hideous light, and I covered my mouth to stifle my gasp as I watched the color drain from the soldier's body. His eyes turned a pure white along with his skin. The zombies released him and he dropped to the ground like a rag doll.

The creatures raised their red eyes to us. Their white lips curled back in long, wide smirks that revealed long, sharp teeth.

Durion floated to the front and beckoned to us. "Come, friends, and revel in a peace greater than we have ever known."

Xander narrowed his eyes. I felt a deep rumble from his chest. "You are no friend of ours, monster."

The creature chuckled. "If you will not be our friend then you will at least be our meal."

The zombies leapt forward. Xander and Cayden stumbled backward away from the clingy claws of the half-rotted corpses. I noticed those who had fed off the soldier had pinker skin beneath their ragged, dirt-covered clothing.

Our dragon lords turned and fled down the path. I glanced over Xander's shoulder and watched the zombies fade into the distance. Even the trees above us stopped blocking the sky.

Xander glanced to his right where Cayden flitted through the trees. "To the sky!"

Cayden nodded, and together their wings exploded from their backs. They flapped hard and we left the ground. We broke through the canopy and flew two hundred feet into the sky before they turned around to face where we'd come.

A large patch of gray surrounded the ancient ruins. It extended in a straight line that followed our path until just beyond where the soldier fell. Even as we watched, however, the path widened as the zombies spread their desecration across the forest. Animals fled through the trees. Those that were caught were drained to death by the zombies. The birds flew up into the sky and retreated into the far horizon.

Cayden looked to us with an ashen face. "How can we stop such evil?"

Xander pursed his lips and shook his head. "I do not know."

"Don't you dragon guys have magic or something? Like what the guys at the Portal?" I reminded them.

"We have a simple magic, but against such a foe I doubt even the most gifted dragon caster would stand a chance," Xander told me.

"What of the vial of tears?" Cayden suggested. "Can one of us not leave here and-" His suggestion was interrupted by a groan from the forest far beneath us.

Xander pressed me tighter to his chest and pursed his lips. "We must return to Keskella and take counsel with the king. He may give us insight into our foes."

# CHAPTER 12

We flew back to the city and reached the northern gate in half the time it took to get to the ruined castle. I heard shouts and the clash of steel, and glanced down. Spiros and the others were in the middle of a fight with the city soldiers.

"Xander!" Cayden yelled.

"We must reach the palace!" he replied.

They flew through the air over the green city. We reached the halfway point when balls of green, crackling light shot up from the rooftops and streets. Xander and Cayden took evasive maneuvers, but one of the balls came close enough that I could feel the scorching heat from its surface.

I spotted our foes. They were more fae guards. The fae charged the weapons in their hands like the possessed Durion had done at the ruins and threw them at us.

"Why are they shooting at us?" I yelled.

Cayden shook his head. "Perhaps they-" His replying meant he didn't focus on the balls around us. One of them hit him square in the center of one wing. I smelled the singed skin from ten yards off and smoke curled up from the point of impact.

Cayden's flapping faltered and he nosedived toward the ground. Stephanie screamed and clung to him as they plummeted.

"Hold tight!" Xander commanded me.

I barely had time to tighten my grip around his neck when he dove after them. We started out at three hundred feet above the ground and reached them halfway to the dead-end point. Xander swooped under Cayden and positioned us beneath our friends. He gritted his teeth and flapped his powerful wings. Cayden fell onto his back and pushed us down, but Xander's wing strokes slowed both our descents.

The ground with its cobblestone hardness came upon us. At ten feet Xander threw himself backward so Cayden slid off his back. The dragon men both landed hard on their feet. They stumbled forward and fell to their knees with we Maidens still clutched tightly in their arms, unharmed but not unfazed.

I slid out of Xander's grasp and spun around to grab his shoulders. His chest moved in and out as he tried to get back his strength. I knelt in front of him and smiled. "That was some trick. Where did you learn to do that?"

He pursed his lips. "In a great war, but we have more pressing matters to attend to."

Those 'pressing matters' were the three dozen guards who popped up out of the stonework and surrounded us. Xander and Cayden climbed to their feet as the leader of the fae guards, the fellow from the tavern stepped up to the front of their ranks. He had a nice shiner, courtesy of Xander's fist.

"Attempt to escape and you will all die," the fae leader warned us.

Xander straightened and scowled at him. "We are not your enemies. We bring news about the-"

"Be quiet," the fae snapped. He nodded his head to a few of his men who marched forward and moved behind Xander and Cayden. They shackled the dragon men with thick iron manacles. "Whatever you have to say can wait until you are in the presence of our king, now move along."

We were marched up the hills to the palace. In the courtyard we found the rest of our companions lined up along the left-hand walkway. They were on their knees with a contingent of guards on either side of them.

Darda straightened and her eyes widened when she beheld us. "My Lord!"

"A moment, Darda," he assured her.

One of the fae behind us shoved him forward. "Not likely," he hissed.

Our group climbed the wide stairs up to the throne room. The elderly fae with their flowing robes awaited us. The king sat regal in his throne, but his hands were pale as they grasped the front of the arms. We were pushed to within ten feet of the throne room and forced onto our knees.

King Thorontur leaned forward and glared at us. "Where is my son?"

Xander raised his head and met the menacing gaze. "Your son has been taken by the restless souls that inhabit the ruined castle. They have used his magic and their ancient fury to raise their bodies from the ground. As we waste our time speaking they drain the forest of its life to replenish their own charred corpses."

Thorontur's eyes widened and he fell back against his seat. The others scoffed.

"Preposterous. Of what ruined castle do you speak?" one of the counselors questioned him.

"Pimeys."

The reply came not from my dragon lord from the king of the forest. All eyes fell on the king who's face was as pale as marble. His hands trembled so badly he clasped them in his lap.

His lead counselor hurried to his side. "Your Highness, what is the matter?"

He stiffened his jaw and shook his head. "But it cannot be. They were destroyed. The gods themselves destroyed them."

"What the gods destroyed vengeance makes anew," Xander told him.

"What are you talking about? Explain yourself!" an adviser ordered the dragon lord.

"The men of old, those who once ruled these woods, have risen from their grave in their ruined city," Xander replied.

Thorontur gritted his teeth and pounded a fist against the arm of the chair. "The dead cannot be raised! They are in their graves until the end of time!"

"Would you doubt our word and your son's absence to gratify your fear?" Xander challenged him.

"The men are gone! They will not rise!" Thorontur insisted.

"You are a fool, Thorontur!" Xander boomed. He spread his wings and knocked the guards away so he could stand. A red hue of light pulsed off his body. The advisers stumbled away from the light. "Open your closed heart to the forest! Hear its cries as the undead take its life! The same will happen to your city and all your people if something is not done!"

"Guards! Guards!" the lead counselor screamed.

The guards regrouped and surrounded Xander. They pointed their long, pointed spears at him and prepared to stab. Xander whipped his head to one group and snarled. The red hue around him thickened and floated off him in waves.

"Enough." The voice that spoke was old and wary. Thorontur raised his hand and shook his head. "Do him no harm." The guards hesitated. Thorontur raised his head and frowned at them. "Lower your weapons!"

They lowered their weapons and stood at attention. Xander, too, lowered his defenses. He let out a long breath and the red glow disappeared. His body relaxed as the king of the woods rose from his seat.

"You are right to berate me, Grand Dragon Lord. I have long felt this illness within the forest, but I chose to hide away in our city in the hopes that this dormant evil would fade." He straightened and stiffened his jaw. "But I will do so no longer. I myself will attempt to purify the defiled ground."

A great roar of disapproval sprang up from the counselors.

"You cannot, sire!"

"If we lose you, all is lost!"

"Surely others may go in your place!"

Thorontur turned and glared at his counselors. "If I do not try, all *will* be lost, and I will not see my son nor my city take the punishment for my failed wisdom."

"But how could such a ritual be performed, and where shall it take place?" one of them pointed out.

Thorontur returned his attention to Xander. "You spoke of their rising from their ruined castle. You traveled to the forbidden part of the forest?"

Xander bowed his head. "We did, Your Highness, and it was there that your son was taken by their vengeful power."

The old king pursed his lips. "Then the cleansing must be performed there, in the heart of their domain. Anything less and the spell may not take effect."

"But sire, how will you reach the center without you yourself being attacked?" one of his counselors pointed out.

"My men and I offer you our assistance," Xander spoke up. "We will fly you and your guards to the spot and guard you as well as we can."

The counselor scoffed at him. "That is the most-"

"Then it is settled," Thorontur agreed. "I will make my preparations and meet you all in the courtyard in ten minutes."

The king's advisers gawked at Thorontur as he walked past us and out the door. The guards hurriedly freed us and marched behind him, leaving us without a chaperon.

Xander looked to Cayden as the rest of us stood. "I will understand if you choose not to follow me into such danger."

Cayden shook his head. "I would not abandon you now, Grand Dragon Lord. Not for all the spices in the world."

Xander smiled and nodded. "Your father smiles down on you this day, brave Dragon Lord." He turned his attention to me and his face fell. My dragon lord clasped our hands together. "You must remain here, Miriam. The danger is too great. If we were to fail-"

"Then I'd be screwed anyway," I finished for him. I managed a shaky smile as I shook my head. "I'm not going to be left behind like some forgotten piece of luggage. Besides, I've always wanted to see how long I'd last battling zombies."

"But you are unarmed," he pointed out.

"And outmatched," a voice spoke up. We turned our attention to the open throne room doors. Tillit leaned against the left-hand door frame with a grin on his face. "Did you miss me?"

My face fell and my eyebrows crashed down. "You're a little late."

He pushed off the door frame and held up his hands. "Give Tillit a little mercy, My Lady. Your lord asked much of me in a short time. Besides-" he tapped the side of his nose and winked at us, "-I might be too late to tell you what the old king knows, but I can tell you what he doesn't know."

Cayden furrowed his brow. "What does King Thorontur not know?"

Tillit jerked his head toward the door. "I talked with the dragon boys and they told me the thing got the prince when he was talking about doing a cleansing. That might be the trick to killing this thing."

"The king will attempt to perform a purification of the ruins," Xander told him.

Tillit smiled and shook his head. "That won't work. It's too weak."

"Is there a difference?" I spoke up.

Tillit nodded. "Yep. One of them's the easy way out. That's the purification magic. It's like pouring water on a knife wound. The other one, the cleansing, is like dumping a barrel of sacred water onto a paper cut."

"So why doesn't the king just use the cleansing?" I asked them.

Xander furrowed his brow. "Cleansing is far more difficult to perform. A single mistake would render the spell powerless, and we would be at the mercy of our foes."

"Which means we'd be dead," I added.

He nodded. "Yes."

I folded my arms over my chest and frowned. "So the king wants to use the easy way just in case he messes up. That doesn't exactly give me confidence in him doing any spells."

"King Thorontur is skilled with the fae magic. He will perform the purification as well as anyone, and if need be he will cleanse the area, as well," Xander assured me. He turned his attention to Tillit. "But is that all you found?"

Tillit grinned. "Always wanting to stretch your coin, My Lord? Though as a matter of fact, I did find something when I was talking to those two crazy fae who live in this tree." His eyes fell on me and he winked. "But I'll have to look into it some more and get back to you. If we survive this monster attack, that is." He bowed deeply to us and stepped back. "Anyway, good luck to you, and may the gods of fortune shine on us all." Tillit turned and strode down the stairs.

I looked to Xander and jerked my head in the direction Tillit had gone. "Is there something in the water here, or is everyone in this world a little weird?"

He pursed his lips. "Some of both, but come. I have little time for preparation."

## CHAPTER 13

"I'm going."

"You are not."

Xander and I walked down the stairs with this unfinished argument still brewing between us. Cayden and Stephanie moved hand-in-hand behind us.

"I told you I'm going," I insisted.

"And I informed you you would remain here," he reminded me.

"I'm going."

"You are not."

"I'm *not* not going."

"You are not."

"Aha!" I slipped in front of Xander and pointed a finger at him. "That means I'm going!"

He frowned. "This is no time for jesting, Miriam. You yourself witnessed the destructive powers of these creatures. You have no ability to protect yourself from their touch."

"And you think your claws are going to work?" I countered.

"They will do better than your inexperience, but I will not argue this matter further." We reached the bottom of the stairs and Xander turned to face me. He set his hands on my shoulders and looked into my eyes. "Whatever happens, know that I only wanted to keep you safe." He leaned forward and pressed a gentle kiss on my forehead.

I reached out for him, but Xander stepped back into the hollow hallway. Cayden gallantly kissed Stephanie's hand and joined Xander. The king and a small entourage of his guards met him in front of the doors, and together they left the tree.

I shook myself from my stupor and hurried after him. The courtyard was filled with fae and dragon soldiers. Spiros and our other soldierly friends stood close to the two dragon lords. The dragons looked on as the fae, the old king included, girdled themselves for battle with short swords and knives.

I slipped behind the dragons to the arched hallway. Xander's eyes flickered over his shoulder and fell on me. He looked to Spiros. "I entrust the safety of my Maiden to you, old friend."

Spiros shook his head. "I refuse to leave you again, My Lord."

Xander frowned. "You would disobey me?"

"I would point out that the fae need as many dragons as can be spared to fly them to the ruins," he pointed out.

My dragon lord pursed his lips and looked ahead. "Very well, but if anything was to happen to me-"

"I will take your Maiden as my bride," Spiros finished with a crooked grin.

A ghost of a smile slipped over Xander's lips, but he didn't have time to reply. King Thorontur stepped up to the dragons. "My men and I are prepared for battle."

"May the gods grant us favor," Xander added as he slipped behind the king.

Xander himself slipped his arms under those of Thorontur and lifted him into the air. The same was done for the other fae, and in a few moments the small group was airborne and over the city. I stepped up to the archway and watched them go until their specks disappeared into the far distance.

Stephanie stepped up behind me and set a hand on my shoulder. "Are you okay?" she whispered.

I turned my face away from her and nodded. My voice was huskier than I liked, but it was firm. "Of course. Why wouldn't I be okay?"

She slid her hand off my shoulder. "I'm going inside. Did you want to come with me?"

I shook my head. "No. I'll be in in a bit, okay?"

"All right." She walked past me and into the western wing of the palace.

The others also cleared the area until only I remained. I leaned my back against the archway and pounded my fist against it.

"Damn it!" Tears streamed down my cheeks and blotted out my vision. I tilted my head back and shut my eyes. "Why'd I have to go and fall for a stupid dragon who can just fly off and leave me behind?"

"My Lady wishes to be with her lord?"

I jumped at the voice and whipped my head to the right. Darda stood a few feet from me. Her steady gaze studied me.

I wiped away the tears and sniffled. "I-it's not that. I just don't want that idiot to ditch me. If something happens to him, there goes my meal ticket."

"You would risk your life to be with him?" she wondered.

I lifted my eyes to the darkening sky in the north. My heart felt like a boulder lay on it. I swallowed the lump in my throat and nodded. "Yeah, I guess I would."

Darda smiled and grasped the edges of her fur coat. She slid out of them and let them drop onto a pile on the ground. "Then I will take My Lady to My Lord."

I looked to her and blinked. "How are you-" Green dragon wings spread from her back. My eyes widened and I pointed a shaking finger at the wings. "H-how'd you do that? Xander said you were from my world."

"A dragon may give their heart to a human, tying their lives together." She curled one wing in front of herself and stroked the smooth fabric. "My husband gave a piece of his heart to me and granted me both a longer life and these beautiful wings."

I took a step toward her. "And you can catch up to Xander with those things?"

She released her wing and shook her head. "No, but I fly you there as fast as my strength will allow."

I smiled and jerked my head toward the courtyard. "That's good enough for me. Let's get started."

Darda lifted me up like the dragon soldiers had done to the fae guards. It was a slower liftoff, but once in the air we soared over the city and northward. I held onto Darda's arms for extra security as we flew over the vast expanse of forest. However, the green canopy wasn't endless.

Ahead of us in the close distance was the evidence of the creatures' destructive march. Gray trees stood as silent testimonials to the zombies' revenge. I instinctively tucked my legs close to my chest and swept my eyes over the area. The forest was as silent as the grave.

"I don't see any of those monsters," I commented to Darda.

"Perhaps they have been vanquished by our lord?" she suggested.

I lifted my head and my eyes fell on the ruined vine mound in the distance. Smoke rose from the ground. I pointed at the spot. "There! Get us over there!"

Darda swooped low over the tops of the trees and sped us over to the clearing. We reached the end of the tree line and a terrible scene of battle burst into view. Hundreds of zombies lined the clearing. Many of them were partially human, but others were still charred skeletal things. They gnashed their teeth at the intruders who stood in the courtyard of the ruined castle.

Our friends, and my dragon lord, stood at the battlements and in the archway that led into the courtyard. Their long blades, staffs, and arrows kept the zombies at bay. At the head of the defenders stood Xander with Cayden and Spiros by his side. Together they hacked and hewed the incoming zombies, but their numbers were too small and the zombies' too great.

Standing in the middle of the courtyard was the fae king, Thorontur. A few of his guards stood by as he pressed his hands together in prayer. The familiar green light of the

Arbor Fae pulsed from between his clasped fingers. His eyes were closed and his lips moved in words I couldn't hear, and probably wouldn't have understood.

"The walls!" one of the fae atop the walls shouted.

Darda jerked to a stop and flapped in place to raise us well above the fray. I squirmed in her grasp and glared up at her. "What are you doing? Let me down there!"

She nodded at the walls. "There, My Lady."

I followed her gaze. A horde of zombies piled atop one another and climbed up the ruined front wall. They swept over the side and attacked the archers who were placed along the walls. The fae only had time to scream before the life-draining hands took theirs. The zombies leapt from the battlements and into the courtyard. Thorontur's guards faced them and beat them back, but they were soon overwhelmed.

Xander and the others rushed back to defend the king, leaving a few of our soldiers to battle the swelling hordes of zombies at the archway. They hacked at the fiends, but couldn't stop the zombies as they piled atop Thorontur. The king disappeared beneath their dozens of bodies, and when the zombies scattered at the point of Xander's blade they revealed Thorontur's drained body.

And that's when Durion showed up.

## CHAPTER 14

Our possessed friend slipped from the woods and floated over to the archway. At his side were the vines of the woods and the zombies of the castle. They overwhelmed the soldiers at the gate, turning them into white corpses which Durion passed without note.

The vines slipped ahead of Durion and coiled around the few who remained, namely Xander, Cayden and Spiros. Xander and Cayden were captured, but Spiros hacked away at his vines and broke through to the dragon lords. He grabbed Xander's vines and tore some of them apart.

"Get away!" Xander ordered him. "Fly!"

"Never again!" Spiros shouted.

A half dozen zombies leapt atop Spiros's back and dragged him away from Xander. They grabbed at his flesh and drained him fro a dozen different points. He was dead in a few seconds.

"Spiros!" Xander cried out as Durion floated toward them.

The battle was over in so brief a moment I didn't have a chance to cry out. Now I did. "Xander! Let me down! Let me get to him!"

"And do what, My Lady? You would die as surely as he," Darda pointed out.

I twisted and turned. "Then I'll die! Just let me-" My struggles broke her grasp on my arms.

I screamed as I dropped the twenty feet to the ground. My feet hit the ground hard and I felt a twist in one ankle that told me my landing wasn't perfect. I stood and limped toward the archway. Several of the zombies turned and hissed at me. I stiffened as they spun around and raced for me.

A shadow swooped down and plucked the zombies off the ground by their collars. Darda held onto them long enough to drop them among their comrades, creating a tangle of squirming legs and arms.

Darda circled around and grabbed my hands to pull me away from the gnashing zombies. "I will land us in the courtyard."

I shook my head. "Just drop me. You've got to warn everybody else."

Darda pursed her lips, but gave a curt nod. "As you wish, My Lady."

"Darda! Take her away from her!" Xander yelled as we sailed over the walls.

"Not on your life!" I shouted back.

I opened my hands and dropped into the courtyard. My injured ankle collapsed under me and I fell to my knees. I looked up and watched Darda fly away. There went my only ride.

"Run, Miriam!" Xander ordered me.

I gave him a shaky smile as I stood up on my shaky legs. "A little too late for that."

"Too late. All too late," Durion murmured as he floated toward Xander.

"One sec, zombo!" I yelled as I limped after him.

Vines wrapped around my legs and tripped me. I fell flat on my face and looked up to see the zombie king reach my dragon lord. Durion looked from Xander to Cayden and back. A smirk curled onto his pale lips. "Such wonderful life. Such beautiful life." He reached up and cupped both Xander and Cayden's cheeks.

I stretched out my hand. "No!"

Too late. The gray spread across their faces and down their bodies. The color of their eyes vanished, replaced with emptiness. Their heads fell back with their mouths agape. The vines slipped away and they dropped limp to the ground.

My body trembled as I shook my head. "No. No!" Durion turned to me. I glared at that stupid grin. "You monster! You fucking monster!"

The possessed prince floated over to me and bent down. He grabbed my neck and lifted me off ground so I swung above him. I pawed at his arm, but his strength was as great as the dragon lords he just drained.

His multitude of voices spoke in a tremble of excitement. "What lovely spirit. What a lovely taste for my children."

# REALMS OF THE DRAGONS

I gasped as his hand cut off my air. My eyes flickered past him at my fallen dragon lord. He lay on his stomach and his ashen-colored body faced me. His eyes were the hollow white of cold death. Hot tears streamed down my face. I felt a cold touch as the zombie king slowly drained my life from me.

One of the tears dropped from my cheek and onto the thing's face. A bright blue light erupted from the spot.

The zombie let out a terrible scream and dropped me onto the ground. I grabbed my neck and coughed on the air that rushed into my starving lungs. The thing's feet fell to the ground as it staggered back and clawed at his face.

I sat up and raised my eyes in time to watch Durion's body explode in a glittering display of the same dazzling color. Thousands of tiny, reflective glittery pieces spread out over the ruins and enveloped everything. The touch of the glitter felt like a warm blanket after a long, cold winter's day.

Thin lines of color stretched from the zombie king's feet and across the ground to Xander and the others. Their bodies were illuminated with the bright blue light which brought the fresh glow of life back to their skin.

The zombies around me weren't so lucky. They threw up their arms and screamed as the glitter rained down on them. Their bodies burst into more glittering color that piled onto the ground. More lines stretched from the piles to the surrounding trees and dipped deep into the forest.

I raised my arm to shield my eyes and blinked hard against the dazzling light. In the middle of the brilliance stood Durion with his arms outstretched above him. His mouth was open in a soundless scream.

My eyes widened as I watched a blue light in the shape of a human stretch from his body. The light floated out of him and over to my spot on the ground where it knelt down in front of me.

I raised my eyes and found a pair of white eyes staring at me from its smooth face. Though the creature didn't have a mouth, I knew it was smiling. It grasped my arms with hands that felt like steamed gloves and leaned down. Our heads touched, and I closed my eyes as I felt a rush of warmth float into me.

The creature sank into my body. A wave of exhaustion followed. My wobbly arms collapsed beneath me and I fell onto my side. The light in the area faded as the last zombie exploded.

Durion came back into view. His skin was once again a lively color. He dropped his arms and crumpled to the ground.

The prince didn't stir, but everyone else did. Xander, the soldiers, Thorontur, everyone sat up and looked around them with wide, blinking eyes.

Xander only had eyes for me. He struggled to his feet and stumbled over to me. The strong dragon lord fell onto his knees by my side and took me into his arms. His voice was hoarse as he looked into my face. "Miriam? Are you well?"

I smiled up at him. "Better than you."

# CHAPTER 15

Spiros staggered to his feet and clutched his head in one hand. His eyes fell on Xander and me. "My Lord, what happened?"

Xander looked up at him and shook his head. "I do not know."

"There was this blue light," I spoke up. I eased myself into a seated position. My head spun. "It made Durion explode like a firecracker and then that kind of spread everywhere."

"Where did such a powerful light come from?" Cayden asked me.

I stared at the ground and furrowed my brow. "I. . .I think it came from me."

The company stared at me with wide, blinking eyes.

"From you?" Xander repeated.

I looked up at him and glared. "I'm not lying. I was- well, I was crying, okay? And then one of my tears fell on Durion's cheek, and everything just went 'boom!' with this bright blue color."

"Your Highness!"

"Sire, please!"

The commotion came from the other side of the courtyard. Half the fae were crowded around their king who struggled to his feet. He shoved aside their helping hands. His eyes were ever on the prone form of his son who lay between us.

"Let me to my son! Let me be, I say!" he commanded them.

He pushed through them and stumbled over to Durion and the small crowd around the young prince. My heart skipped a beat as Thorontur dropped to his knees beside his son and rolled him over. Durion's face was pale, but not as pale as before.

Thorontur grabbed his son's shoulders and shook him. "My son, awaken! Durion, do you hear me?"

Durion's eyes fluttered open. He smiled up at his dad. "Father. It is good to see your face."

Tears sprang to Thorontur's eyes as he hugged his son. "My son. My dear boy. I thought I would never see you again."

"As did I, and we have much to thank the fair Lady Miriam for," Durion commented.

Thorontur pulled them apart and furrowed his brow. "Of whom and what do you speak, Durion?"

Durion turned and nodded at me. "That is the Lady Miriam, Maiden to the dragon lord Xander. While possessed,

I was able to watch all that occurred. It was she alone who was able to vanquish the evil."

"But how?" Thorontur asked him.

Durion climbed to his feet and leaned heavily on one of the fae soldiers. "Lady Miriam, if you would oblige me by coming over here."

I looked up at Xander. He nodded. I swallowed the lump in my throat and stood on my shaky legs. My ankle was already swollen, but with Xander's help I got over to the weak prince.

Durion held up his hand. The familiar green glow appeared. "If you would place your palm against mine."

I raised my hand and pressed my hand against his. My eyes widened when a blue light appeared from my hand. The fae around us whispered excitedly.

I whipped my head left and right at the curious faces. "Is this a good thing?"

Durion lowered his hand and smiled. "Very good. It proves you are of the Mare Fae."

I blinked at him. "So you're saying those two mad scientists were right?"

Durion tilted his head to one side. "'Mad scientists?'"

I nodded. "Yeah, those two fae guys you and Xander left me with to get rid of my cold. They said I was a fae."

The prince chuckled and bowed his head. "Then yes, I believe they were right."

"Prince, Your Highness, fae and dragons," Xander spoke up. "If I may interrupt this interesting , but these ruins hold some rather unfortunate memories I would like to leave well behind me, or at least as far as Keskella. And there is the matter of the setting sun." He looked up at the sky and its dark colors.

Thorontur nodded. "Yes. We shall leave this terrible place and let it fall into its final rest."

Our large party of injured and dazed straggled out of the courtyard and into the meadow. A smile spread across my face as I gazed out over the rejuvenated forest. The trees and grasses were once again a lush green. A soft breeze rustled through the woods and past us, making it seem as though the trees waved and cheered at us.

A shadow emerged from the woods. It was the first soldier we lost. He stumbled into the clearing and blinked against the harsh light of the setting sun.

"Liam!" Cayden shouted.

The soldier turned to us and we could see his smile even from that distance. "My Lord!"

Our reunion party was brief. Nobody wanted to stay in the shadow of the ruined city. Our going was slow. None of the dragons were in any shape to fly themselves back to the city, much less carry the fae with them.

I hobbled my way along until Xander swept me into his arms and smiled down at me. "If I could not be your savior before, allow me to be your crutch this moment."

I leaned against his chest and enjoyed the warmth. "I'm not going to argue with that."

Xander set his eyes on his captain who walked on his left. "Spiros, I wish to speak with you about a grave matter."

His captain bowed his head to Xander. "I am at your service, My Lord."

"There was something important lacking in your actions this day, and the neglect must be punished," Xander told him.

Spiros arched an eyebrow and pursed his lips. "How have I failed you, My Lord?"

"I didn't see that mead prepared for me when I reached the other side."

The corners of the captain's lips curled up in a smile. "You hardly gave me a chance to find a glass, My Lord."

I looked from one to the other. "So did you guys really die?"

Xander shook his head. "Not in the true sense. Our lives were separated from our bodies and dispersed throughout the rotten corpses. We could still feel ourselves, but over a very wide distance."

I wrinkled my nose. "That doesn't sound like fun."

Xander chuckled. "No. It was rather like being imprisoned in a dark, rotten cage without hope of escape." His eyes studied me and he smiled. "But you gave us hope, and freedom."

I blushed and squirmed in his grasp. "All I did was cry."

"The purest tears washes away all evil," Spiros philosophized.

"And the tears of a Mare Fae are some of the purest," Cayden spoke up as he looked at me. "Those were the same that cured Xander."

I furrowed my brow. "So that means the water guy I met in the river was what? My uncle?"

"He saw you as such," Xander agreed.

I grinned. "I'll have to thank him for not hitting on me, but after I take a long nap."

We reached the fae city a few hours later and found the place a veritable fortress. The men at the gate peeked out from their battlements and gawked at our group as we emerged from the trees. Their shouts of joy rang over the walls.

"Sire!"

"Your Highness!"

"Prince Durion!"

The gate was flung open and the guards poured out. We were escorted in triumph into Metsan Keskella, and a great din arose from all the buildings. I finally got to see how many fae lived in that city. I didn't count them, but I could tell they weren't going to have a population shortage any time soon.

Among the revelers was the rest of our party. Darda and her husband hurried down the hilly street to us.

"My Lord! My Lady!" she cried out as she grasped my hand.

Xander sternly looked at her. "Darda, you knowingly endangered my Maiden."

The servant shrank beneath his gaze and bowed her head. "I understand, My Lord. If you wish to punish me, I am at your mercy."

A teasing smile slipped onto Xander's lips as he shook his head. "There will be no punishment. For this once, I am very grateful for your disobedience."

Darda raised her head and smiled. "I am glad, My Lord."

"But do not make a habit of it," he scolded her.

She bowed her head. "Certainly not, My Lord."

We pressed through the crowds and arrived at the palace. Good news had traveled fast, and the place was practically deserted. There was only one figure, and they leaned a shoulder against the doorway into the tree.

"Greetings, victors!" Tillit greeted us. He pushed off the frame and bowed low. "May I be the one thousandth person to congratulate you on saving all of Viridi Silva?"

"Only Miriam deserves such praise," Xander corrected him.

Tillit raised his head and his eyes shone with a mischievous light. "Indeed. My Lady has shown her true, *blue* colors, has she?"

I glared at him. "How'd you know?"

Tillit pretended to be aghast. "My Lady, did you doubt my skills?"

My face fell. "Those two crazy fae told you, didn't they?"

The Sus chuckled. "Guilty as charged, My Lady."

Xander looked down at me. "If you will excuse us, we wish to retire."

I wrapped my arms tighter around his neck and pecked a kiss on his cheek. "Amen to that."

# CHAPTER 16

Our room was a spacious mix of airy windows, shimmering clean walls, and wood furniture with a stone floor. I slept like a log and didn't open my eyes until well after the sun had risen. A call from the windows caught my attention. I creaked open one eye. Xander's place in the bed was empty. That guy had the energy of a wild stallion.

I sat up and rubbed my eyes. There was another call. "My Lady!"

I slipped off the bed and moved to one of the windows that looked out on the street. The cobblestone way was wall-to-wall packed with people, and they all looked up at my window. When they saw me a great cheer rang up. I started back just as the door to the bedroom opened.

Darda stepped inside with a tray of fruit in her hands. "Good morning, My Lady."

I pointed at the window and the fae below it. "Who are they?"

"The fae, My Lady," she told me as she set the tray on a small table between me and the door.

"But why are they at my window?" I persisted.

"They heard it was My Lady who saved the city, and wish to give their thanks," she explained.

I leaned toward the window and craned my neck. Another call arose from the crowd. I jerked back and turned to Darda. "I don't have to make a speech, do I?"

She smiled and shook her head. "No, My Lady, but His Highness wishes to speak with you once you are dressed."

I looked past her at the door. "Do you know where Xander wandered off to?"

"He wished to speak with the fae healers, and would return in a short while," she told me. "Now if My Lady would please hold still, we must dress you appropriately."

I glanced down at myself. My clothes were stained green with the castle ruins grass. I grinned and looked up at Darda. "I think the king would appreciate me wearing his colors."

"My Lady that is hardly a suitable-" The door opened and my errant dragon lord stepped inside. Darda turned to him. "My Lord, My Lady refuses-"

"-to be dressed up like a doll," I finished for her.

Xander smiled. "It is all right, Darda. After her heroism I do not think King Thorontur would have any qualms with her walking naked before him, though I would. Besides, there isn't time

I slipped past my nurse and joined him at his side. He led me from the room and down the stairs to the courtyard. The gate into the castle was shut, but I could see my adoring fans beyond the metal grates. They yelled and waved to me, and I meekly waved back.

"They are calling you the Neito Vedesta," Xander told me.

I looked up into Xander's mischievous face and raised an eyebrow. "And that means what?"

"Maiden of the Water."

"Do they know it was just a fluke?" I asked him.

He shook his head. "Neither they, nor I, know that. It was your compassion that granted your tears, and if one's character is a 'fluke' then my upbringing has greatly deceived me."

I studied him with a careful eye. "Maybe it has, but what were you doing with those two crazy elves?"

"I was merely ascertaining how such an obvious heritage was overlooked by so many, even yourself."

"And?"

"They are at a loss to explain your hidden blood."

"So they might be wrong?" I suggested.

He chuckled. "Your modesty suits you, but in this case it also clouds your judgment. There is an impartial judge to your actions, as well, and he vouches for your noble heritage."

By this time we had reached the top of the stairs that led to the throne room. A pair of guards opened the doors and we stepped into the large chamber. Dozens of elegantly dressed fae lined the walls on either side of us with the soldiers, decked out in their finest, stood before the crowd like a colorful barrier. A great buzz sounded from the crowds as we walked into the room.

Thorontur was seated on his throne. On his right stood Durion. My face fell when I noticed that Alyan and Utiradien stood on the other side of the throne.

"Who let them out..." I murmured.

King Thorontur rose and the murmuring silenced. We stopped before him and knelt on one knee. He smiled and shook his head. "No. Not for you, Lady Miriam, nor you, Grand Dragon." He stooped and grasped one of each of our hands and pulled us to our feet. The old king looked a dozen years younger as he studied my face. "My dear cousin, you have saved more than my kingdom. You have saved my son, and in so doing myself. We ask that you accept this small token of gratitude." He half-turned and swept his hand toward the pair of evil elves.

Alyan and Utiradien stepped forward. Utiradien carried a box covered in green velvet. Alyan opened the lid and pulled out a small glass vial. Within the vial was a tiny green light. Alyan handed the vial to his king who turned to me and held out the gift.

"For you, Lady Miriam, a source of our power."

I took the vial and looked at the small, pulsing ball of light. It looked like a glowing marble. "Um, thanks. It's very pretty."

"May it guide you wherever you go," Thorontur replied.

Xander looped his arm through mine and turned us around so we faced the crowd. Cheers erupted from the company. Flowers were tossed in our direction. I felt like we'd just taken our wedding vows.

Thorontur raised his arms above his head. "Now let us continue our celebrations!"

The soldiers stepped aside for the crowds to pass. Xander led me to the side and we bowed our heads to the whole company as they passed. By the time we were done I knew what a bobble-head doll felt like.

Contrary to custom, Thorontur was the last to leave. He grasped Xander's hand. "Will you not join in the festivities?"

Xander shook his head. "We cannot. I have been too long away from my kingdom, and have ordered my men to leave this very day."

"Then I shall thank you again for saving my own kingdom," Thorontur replied. His eyes fell on me and he grasped my hands together. "Thank you, cousin. With all my heart, I thank you."

"And I must give my thanks as well," Durion spoke up.

I smiled and nodded. "You're both welcome. And thanks for the gift."

He chuckled. "I hope it has some use for you. If you will excuse me."

They followed the others down the stairs. Xander and I were alone. I held up the glass vial and looked at the glowing ball. "So what is this thing, anyway? It looks like the glowing balls they used to light the halls."

"What you hold is far more precious than the firefly lamps around the city. The essence of a fae is contained in that vial," Xander told me.

The color drained from my face as I whipped my head to stare up at him. "Like somebody's soul?"

He smiled. "Yes. The fae have an abundance of life granted to them by the gods of old, and so are able to gift parts of themselves to others." He nodded at the vial. "What you hold is a part of the king's soul captured within a soul stone."

I cringed and looked back at the stone. "So what happens if I drop it?"

Xander chuckled. "Soul stones cannot be broken."

"And I do what with it?"

"Carry it with you and when you are in danger, use its powers to defend yourself," he told me.

I snorted. "So I'm going to what? Blind a guy with it?"

He offered me his arm. "Every soul stone is different, but let us enjoy some quiet before we leave."

I tucked the vial in one pocket and took Xander's arm. "I thought you'd never ask."

# CHAPTER 17

Xander led me downstairs where we met Tillit. The Sus smiled and bowed to us. "Good morning, good morning! I think I can make it a better one for you by leading you out the servant's entrance of the palace. Otherwise, you're liable to get trampled to death with appreciation."

"We would be grateful for the alternate route," Xander agreed.

"Then follow Tillit!"

Tillit led us through the eastern wing of the palace and out through a door nudged against the tree. We stepped out onto a side street that wound its way down to a small park.

Tillit stepped away from us and bowed again. "If Tillit can ever be of service to you again, My Lord, just ring me up at the old Sus Tavi."

"Then you are returning to Alexandria?" Xander guessed.

Tillit straightened and nodded. "Yep. Home beckons me, and I will obey its sweet siren call." Stepped back and saluted us. "God speed, you two, and try not to get into too much trouble without Tillit."

The strange little Sus slipped away down the street and out of sight. I looked up into Xander's face. "You know the strangest people."

He chuckled as he guided me down the street to the small, green park with its shade trees and grass. "A man of the world must know the world and all its oddities."

"And you know *all* its oddities," I teased as I dropped onto the grass. The vial rattled in my pocket. I pulled it out and studied the contents. "You think my soul looks green or blue?"

"All Mare Fae have a blue aura, and thus a blue-colored soul," Xander told me as he took a seat beside me.

I clasped the vial in both hands and turned to Xander. "Those two weird fae told me there were four kinds of fae. Other than where they live, are they pretty much the same?"

He shook his head. "No. The elements under their control are different, as is their interactions with others. The Rus, Mons, and Arbor fae interact quite often with other species and have a large population while the Mare Fae, what you are, is the rarest and most secluded of the four kinds."

"But I've seen two of the Mare in two different spots," I pointed out.

"They have appeared in your presence, no doubt because they sensed one of their own in you," he told me.

"So are they the weakest? You know, being stuck in water and all."

He shook his head. "On the contrary. A mountain may be chipped away, a forest cut down, or the fields burned, but what can one do with water?"

I shrugged. "Dam it?"

He chuckled. "True, but is the water not still there? And does it not still run over the dam and continue on its journey?"

I looked down at myself. "So how come I'm not stuck in water like the other two? And how come I was in my world and not here?"

"That is indeed an interesting question, and the answers will show why you are different."

I drew my legs against my chest and wrapped my arms around them. "Well, I don't *feel* any different."

Xander smiled. "Nor would I have you be so. You are perfect the way you are."

I couldn't help but smile myself. "Flattery will get you everywhere." I tilted my head back and admired the sunlight that filtered through the branches like yellow rainbows. "This place isn't so bad when it's not trying to kill us."

Xander slipped behind me and draped his arms over mine. His warm breath wafted over my neck and his words tingled my ear. "Not as beautiful as you."

Somebody cleared their throat. I whipped my head around so fast my forehead knocked into Xander's nose. He jerked back and clasped his bruised nose in his hand.

I saw Spiros standing a few feet away with a wide grin on his face. The captain bowed to us. "I apologize for the intrusion, but the company is ready to leave."

"Your apology is accepted, but only this time," Xander snuffled. He stood and helped me to my feet. "Are you prepared for another adventure, Miriam?"

I pocketed the vial and grinned. "Definitely."

And what a dozy that one would be.

# A note from Mac

Thank you for purchasing my book! Your support means a lot to me, and I'm grateful to have the opportunity to entertain you with my stories.

If you'd like to continue reading the series, or wonder what else I might have up my writer's sleeve, feel free to check out my website at *macflynn.com*, or contact me at mac@macflynn.com.

*\*\**

Want to get an email when the next book is released? Sign up for the Wolf Den, the online newsletter with a bite, at *eepurl.com/tm-vn*!

# Continue the adventure

Now that you've finished the book, feel free to check out my website at **macflynn.com** for the rest of the exciting series.

Here's also a little sneak-peek at the next book:

*Labyrinth of the Dragon:*

"Are we there yet?"
Regrettably, the whine came from me, but I had to blame my butt. After eight days of travel it was hanging by a thread to what was left of my jostled spine.
"Nearly there," Xander assured me.
I glanced around at the scenery and our shrunken party. Cayden and Stephanie had separated from us after we exited through the southern part of Viridi Silva. The scenery had changed with their passing. Gone were the vast expanses of rolling, tree-covered hills of the High Castle and woods, and in their place was a landscape of short stony mountains and small glens. Winding strips of trees broke the landscape and signaled that one of dozens of smalls creek supplied water to the cottages that dotted the hills. The water ended at small ponds where farm animals lapped up the precious resource.
"So what's going to happen when we do get to this city of yours?" I asked him.

He smiled. "You will be presented as my Maiden before my people and trained in your responsibilities."

I raised an eyebrow. "What responsibilities?"

"As Maiden to me, you are queen of my kingdom. You will manage the palace and address any problems that arise therein," he explained.

The color drained from my face. "Run the palace? I haven't even run a business."

Xander chuckled. "Do not feel anxious. Darda and many others will assist you."

The road we traveled was a wide, hard-packed dirt way. We passed many carts as they rolled along in the same direction as our little group. Many of the drivers pulled to the side of the road and bowed their heads at Xander. He smiled and returned the gesture.

"So does everybody know what you look like?" I asked him.

He shook his head. "No, but they are aware only those of my house are allowed to bear the crest of my family."

"And how many people are in your house?"

"It is only I who remain of the main branch, but I have a family of distant cousins who I have granted use of the coat. Unfortunately, you are little likely to see them for they do not reside in the city, but live abroad."

My face fell. "That sounds kind of lonely."

Xander smiled. "My duties keep me preoccupied. Do you have any siblings?"

I shook my head. "No, but there's my parents. They're divorced, but I still see both of them."

He arched an eyebrow. "'Divorced?'"

"Yeah. Don't you guys get divorces over here?" I wondered.

"What does it mean?"

"Well, it means they're not married anymore," I explained to him.

Xander furrowed his brow. "We do not have that custom here. If one marries, they marry for life."

I snorted. "That means you dragon lords take a big risk on the Maidens, don't you? You could be stuck with someone you don't like."

He smiled at me. "I am grateful I will not have to consider this 'divorce.'"

I shifted in my saddle and winced. "Speaking of divorces, my butt's about to divorce itself from the rest of me. How far is it?"

Xander nodded at a long, gentle slope in front of us. "Alexandria is just over that hill."

I craned my neck as we climbed the hill and peeked over the ridge. There, laid out on a small plain, was the city of Alexandria. The metropolis abutted a large lake fed by the snow-capped mountains to its northwest. The late morning sun in the east cast a dazzling glow on the white stone buildings with their timbered and shingled roofs. Steeples pierced the skyline, and a large square opened in the very center of the grid. The whole of the city was protected by a tall stone wall fifty feet high and half as thick. A single wide gate allowed entrance into the city.

The lake was nearly round with an active harbor filled with dozens of docks large and small. Sailing ships were anchored near the harbor, and smaller boats littered the docks. A small island sat some hundred yards out and was connected to the mainland by a narrow strip of land. Trees covered its otherwise rocky shore, and I could see a large white obelisk near the far shore with a small stone building situated at its base.

The palace of my dragon lord was a majestic fortress of white stone situated along the northwest shore of the lake. It had four terraces that climbed halfway up the steep, white-stoned mountain. A gate at the bottom-most terrace had fifty feet of lake-front property before a long dock stretched out into the waters in the direction of the city.

Xander paused and studied me. "What do you think of it?"

"Wow," I breathed.

He chuckled. "I am glad to hear you say so."

I swallowed my amazement and nodded at the castle. "That must be pretty easy to defend."

"In six thousand years, it has never been taken by outside forces," he told me.

I arched an eyebrow. "What about inside ones?"

He pursed his lips and tugged on the reins of his steed. "Unfortunately, my family has not been immune to internal strife. But come. I am eager to see my home from a closer distance."

We carried on and in a half hour had reached the gate. The archway towered thirty feet above our heads, and the two wood doors, made of six-inch thick boards nailed together with metal bands, were twenty feet wide. They were thrown open to the many carts, wagons and pedestrians that streamed in and out of the gate.

Three guards on either side had their backs to the arch and watched all who came and went. There was a small wood door in the left pillar of the arch. The guards noticed our regal group and stood at greater attention. Spiros rode up to the doorway and dismounted. The guard closest to the door knocked on the entrance.

A man stepped out and looked around. He wore the armor of a soldier but with a crooked, ragged felt cap on his head of shocking red hair. Perched on his shoulder was a small, gray-and-white hawk with alert yellow eyes.

Spiros smiled as the man saluted him. "How goes, captain?"

A crooked smile slipped onto the man's lips and he saluted Spiros. "Better now that you're back, Spiros. You can take the blame for my mistakes."

Spiros cleared his throat and jerked his head over his shoulder. The captain looked past him at us. His face fell and straightened a little more before he bowed. "Greetings, My Lord!"

His proclamation caught the attention of everyone around us. The pedestrians stepped back and gawked while the cart drivers hurried past to make room.

Xander smiled and bowed to him. "Greetings, Kinos. I see the city still stands."

Kinos nodded. "It does, My Lord, but she shimmers now that you have returned."

Xander turned his horse toward the long street in front of us. "I shall make the inspection myself, and if I should find a blemish I will give you the lash."

"Spare some for my commander, now that he has returned," Kinos added with a sly look at Spiros.

"I will do so," Xander agreed, and with a bow of their heads we headed off. Spiros jumped onto his horse and followed behind.

I leaned toward Xander. "Who was that?"

"Kokinos is the captain of the city," he told me.

I glanced over my shoulder at Spiros. "Isn't Spiros in charge of that?"

Xander shook his head. "No. Spiros leads the castle guards and my personal retinue, and Kokinos does report to Spiros."

"But you called him something else. Kino?" I guessed.

He smiled. "Kinos is merely a nickname. His true name is Kokinos."

"And does that mean anything?"

"It refers to the color red in the ancient Alexandrian language. Kinos's family is legendary for their hair."

I looked around us at the broad cobblestone street. On either side were two-story houses made of dried brick, some with open shops for their bottom floor and others used completely for housing. Their walls were whitewashed to perfection and many had flower pots beside their wood doorways. Chimneys puffed out smoke from kitchen stoves and warmed the streets with wondrous smells. Over many of the doorways were carved a sword of stone.

However, I couldn't help but notice the many stares we received. People stepped aside and bowed to us. The travelers in their cloaks gawked at our presence. Children leaned out their windows and waved to us. Some of them peeked out far enough for a necklace to dangle out from their necks. On the end of the jewelry was the same sword design as over the houses.

"So is this how much attention all your walks through town get?" I asked him.

"And sometimes a great deal more," he replied.

I shrank beneath all those staring eyes and curious faces. The main road traveled through the large city square I had seen from the hill. An enormous fountain with three tiers sat in the center. Covered stalls lined around the perimeter of the circular square and people hawked wears of all kinds. There were fabrics, fruits, furniture, and small animals.

One small animal was familiar, and over our heads. A white hawk flew over us in the direction of the castle. I pointed at the bird. "Isn't that-"

"Kinos's own hawk. He takes news of our arrival to the castle," Xander explained to me.

"I wish it'd take me. . ." I mumbled.

We rode through the square and back down the main street to the docks. The bustle of activity wasn't slowed by our arrival. Crews loaded and unloaded boxes, crates, and all sorts of smaller objects and officials with clipboards made tallies of the wares coming and going.

Our retinue rode to the longest and most pristine dock in the whole of the harbor. It stretched into the water for two hundred feet, and tied to one of the tall posts was an elegant sailing ship. The ship was fifty feet long and half that distance wide. Its shimmering wooden masts matched the white sheets of its sails. At the head of its bow was a mermaid with a naked upper torso and a fish tail.

The deck and dock had a tough-looking crew with patched clothes and a few of them with scars on their arms and faces. One of them was a scraggly fellow with an eye-patch and a grizzled gray beard.

He waved a finger at one of the crew on deck, a man in a clean outfit. "Watch yerself there, sir! Keep your wits about you!"

The man sneered and waved his hand. "Ah knows, sir, Ah knows!" He picked up a wood box and walked to the gangplank. His foot slipped on a puddle of water and he crashed onto his rear.

The grizzled man shook his head and glanced in our direction. He squinted his eyes for a moment and a smile broke through his whiskers. "Well, well, look what the land rats brought to us."

Xander dismounted and the rest of us followed suit. "Good day, Captain Magnus. I hope the winds are favorable."

The captain limped over to us and nodded his head. "The winds are always temperamental, Yer Lordship, but today they are smiling on ye." His eyes fell on me and his bushy gray eyebrows shot up. "What have we hear? Has Yer Lordship caught his fish of the sea?"

Xander half turned and gestured to me. "Captain Magnus Heinason, allow me to introduce you to my Maiden, Miriam Cait."

The captain bowed his head. "It's a pleasure to meet ya, My Lady. His Lordship's caught a fine fish, a very fine fish."

Xander nodded at the ship. "Is she sea-worthy, Captain?"

Magnus followed his gaze and grinned. "Aye, but for some landed fish on the crew. Some of me sailors went and abandoned ship for a better port at Bruin Bay, but I say 'bah' to them! None good pickings of ladies there, the fools!" His eyes flickered to me and he coughed into his hand. "That is, none good work to be got there, Yer Lordship."

"May we board, Captain?" Xander asked him.

The captain stepped aside and swept his hand to the ship. "Of course, Yer Lordship, of course! Come aboard, ye and all yer men!"

# Other series by Mac Flynn

*Contemporary Romance*
Being Me
Billionaire Seeking Bride
The Family Business
Loving Places
PALE Series
Trapped In Temptation

*Demon Romance*
Ensnare: The Librarian's Lover
Ensnare: The Passenger's Pleasure
Incubus Among Us
Lovers of Legend
Office Duties
Sensual Sweets
Unnatural Lover

*Dragon Romance*
Blood Dragon
Dragon Bound
Maiden to the Dragon

*Ghost Romance*
Phantom Touch

### *Vampire Romance*
Blood Thief
Blood Treasure
Vampire Dead-tective
Vampire Soul


### *Urban Fantasy Romance*
Death Touched


### *Werewolf Romance*
Alpha Blood
Alpha Mated
Beast Billionaire
By My Light
Desired By the Wolf
Falling For A Wolf
Garden of the Wolf
Highland Moon
In the Loup
Luna Proxy
Marked By the Wolf
Moon Chosen
The Moon and the Stars
Moon Lovers
Oracle of Spirits
Scent of Scotland: Lord of Moray
Shadow of the Moon
Sweet & Sour
Wolf Lake

Manufactured by Amazon.ca
Bolton, ON